# CHASING
# THE BLUE SKY

## WILL LOWREY

# CHASING THE BLUE SKY

Copyright © 2018 by William C. Lowrey

*First Edition*

Editing by 29 Pilgrims Editorial Services and Kassie R. Tibbott

Formatting and Cover Design by The Book Khaleesi

ISBN 978-1-7329399-0-5 (paperback)

LOMACK
PUBLISHING

www.lomackpublishing.com

# TABLE OF CONTENTS

List of Characters............................................................ vii
Chapter 1......................................................................1
Chapter 2....................................................................21
Chapter 3....................................................................35
Chapter 4....................................................................44
Chapter 5....................................................................56
Chapter 6....................................................................74
Chapter 7....................................................................87
Chapter 8....................................................................96
Chapter 9...................................................................113
Chapter 10.................................................................133
Chapter 11.................................................................142
Chapter 12.................................................................151
Chapter 13.................................................................165
Epilogue ...................................................................179
About the Author .......................................................181

*To the forgotten ones — on chains, in kennels, and concrete catacombs —and every person who has ever given a piece of their soul to save them.*

# LIST OF CHARACTERS

- *Alex* – Dog; Corgi mix
- *Allison* – Human female teenager; Clay County Animal Shelter volunteer
- *Anne* – Human woman; Clay County Animal Shelter staff
- *Brutus* – Dog; Mutt
- *Derrick* – Human man; Clay County Animal Shelter staff
- *Dizzy Dean* – Dog; Pit bull type
- *Dmitri* – Dog; Mutt
- *Fiona* – Dog; Pit bull type
- *Frankie* – Dog; Terrier/Collie mix
- *House Wren* - Bird
- *Jack* – Dog; Great Dane/Mastiff mix
- *Julius* – Dog; Pit bull type
- *Katie* – Human female teenager; Clay County Animal Shelter volunteer
- *Leonard* – Dog; Beagle
- *Lexi* – Dog; Hound
- *Marilynn* – Dog; Young Golden Retriever
- *Mason* – Human boy
- *Melissa* – Human woman; Clay County Animal Shelter staff
- *Mother* – Dog; Pit bull type; Toby's mother
- *Oscar* – Dog; Pit bull type/Mastiff mix
- *Peter* – Human father

- *Roland* – Human man; Clay County Animal Shelter staff
- *Ruby* – Dog; Chocolate Labrador Retriever
- *Sadie* – Dog; Border Collie mix
- *Samantha* – Human girl
- *Sandra* – Human mother
- *Squirrel* – Woodland creature
- *Susan* – Human woman; Clay County Animal Shelter Director
- *Toby* – Dog; Pit bull type
- *Zeke* – Dog; Black Labrador Retriever mix

# CHAPTER 1

T here is no greater hunter than the sun.

No matter what the little dog did, she could not escape it. The searing rays stalked her every movement, twist, and contortion. The brutal heat soaked relentlessly into the warm depths of her dirty white coat.

Lifting her chin from the hard, rotted wood of the doghouse floor, she pushed and slid her body back into a corner with a gentle, defeated grunt. The points of a dozen dirty splinters dug into her soft, pink underside, the pain going unnoticed in her desperate pursuit of shade. Her puppies moved with her, wriggling and squirming to follow her bulging nipples.

She put her head down and let out a long sigh as the heat baked through the crumbling roof, through the cracked floor, and through the wide entryway, engulfing her in an unquenchable misery. Even her thick, metal chain was hot; the end of it was nailed unceremoniously to the front of her doghouse, constantly exposed to the summer heat and acting as a conductor for the remainder of its length. She did her best to keep from brushing the chain, although occasionally one of the puppies would whelp in pain as the scorching metal brushed against their young, fresh skin. On days like today, she longed for the times before the chain.

Long ago, there was a plastic-coated wire. Its length allowed her several more feet to explore, and the plastic kept the heat from burning her as the chain so often did. But then her people got rid of the wire, and she never saw it again.

She remembered that day well, the day they got rid of the wire. Early that morning, she had tangled herself around the tree. She sat there all day at the base of the oak tree, pulled taut against the dry bark. She didn't know how to get out of her predicament, and after an hour of spinning and barking, she finally sat to rest at the base of the tree and waited for her people. The wire pulled tightly against her collar for many hours.

The man had come home first that day as he often did, and she let out a short yelp to let him know she was there as he often forgot. After some time passed, he came into the yard, his work boots kicking up dust as he descended the old wooden steps of the deck.

She was happy to see the man, but the man did not look happy in return. The dark crease of a frown crossed his rugged chin, his brow furrowed like a pair of caterpillars.

She remembered being tugged hard against the tree, the tether yanking at her neck and her snout scraping into the bark as her mind raced to understand what was happening. The man was yelling at her and

2

she grew scared. Her ears tucked back, and she scrambled to do what the man wanted, but she was tangled and confused. She continued to scrape against the tree, fighting to keep her legs from twisting under her. Around and around the tree she went until she scraped no more and flopped to the ground in the dust.

The man stood over her now, his figure casting a long, black shadow across the length of her frightened form. He held the tether — which was still attached to her neck — in one hand. His shouts punctuated the early evening, and she blinked her eyes and folded her ears, looking away from the man. She did not want to be here right now. She did not want the man to be mad. She was sorry for what she had done though she didn't know what.

She remembered only dashing heartily after the small brown squirrel with its bushy white tail. She longed to run after him, to chase him wildly and freely around the soft, verdant grass of the yard. Around and around she had gone as the little creature circled and scrambled up the bark of the large tree, his long claws effortlessly scaling higher and higher. And then the tether had pulled taut, a sudden reminder that she was not free like the wild one she chased.

The man's rough face grew flush with anger. He must be mad because she chased the squirrel, she thought. She wouldn't chase the squirrel anymore. He yelled once more, his tone even more irate than before, and gave a sharp tug of the tether. The little white dog's neck ached as it jerked violently towards him.

With that, he released the tether and turned back towards the house, walking quickly away. The determined stomping of his work boots caused a gentle vibration in the dry ground below.

She was scared now and sat motionlessly on her back, her belly exposed, and her legs folded haphazardly. As the man walked up the stairs of the deck, she slowly rolled towards the house and watched him enter, the door slamming behind him. She lay for several more minutes before she dared to sit upright, still looking at the house. Her tail was tucked between her legs, and her ears remained pinned. Her body shivered deep within. She was so sorry she had upset the man.

After a few moments, the door opened once more, the thin aluminum blinds on the window flipping and smacking into each other as the door was yanked quickly backward. The man stormed down the stairs at her once more. In one hand, he held a hammer, in the other, a short, thick metal chain. He was before her in a few strides, pounding one end of the chain and a large nail ferociously into the side of her doghouse. The little white dog sat motionless, daring only a sideways glance at the man as she continued to shiver, and he continued to pound at the doghouse.

The hammering stopped, and the man followed the length of chain to its end and snatched her collar, unclipping the long wire. She heard a metallic click and the man walked away, taking her wire with him. The door slammed behind him once again, its dull echo reverberating across the still yard.

# CHASING THE BLUE SKY

For several long, long minutes, she sat motionless, waiting for the man to come back again. The evening turned to night, but the man did not come back. Finally, the little white dog walked cautiously towards the tree; perhaps she could hide behind its trunk tonight and then tomorrow, things would be better. Suddenly, the collar tugged against her throat and she stopped. Looking back, she saw the rusty chain pulled tight against the doghouse — unforgiving. Her wire was gone. Her tree was gone. Her world had been suddenly cut in half. She looked towards her tree, high up in the branches. Somewhere up there was that squirrel, she thought, watching her down here on the end of a very, very short chain.

And from that point forward, there she sat, alone in the confines of her tiny dominion. The entire scope of her world was now defined by a few dozen links of rusted chain. The days since had passed so slowly.

Today was no different. Morning faded into afternoon as the sun rose high in the sky, perpetually unforgiving in its bright glow. The little white dog had spent every day the same way for as long as she could remember for her two years on this Earth. She often wondered how many days she would sit. How many times would the sun rise and set before she would be no more? *How much longer do I have to stay here in this world of dust, and bugs, and rain, and sun?* she often pondered, casting her dark yellow eyes skyward for an answer that was always the same — another day just like the last.

The summer months were hard and long. The days dragged on mercilessly. Time was an endless pulse on her insufferable existence. Many days, a cool bowl of water, a bone to chew, or a few minutes of time with her people would have been magical. These moments proved to be the exception, though, and her bowl often remained dry, the rusted brown bottom clearly visible in its emptiness. Some mornings when the air was still moist, she would lick the precious drops of condensation from her bowl, from the floor of her house, and from the grass itself. Other times, the heat was dry and crisp, and she went days without water. On many days, the bugs would visit her bowl — big brown spiders and scurrying black beetles crawled across the rim and deep into the bottom. At first, she had tried to chase them away, rattling the bowl with her nose to scare them off, but eventually, she gave up. The bugs were as constant as the sun, and neither listened to her pleas.

In those hot summer months, she cherished the days when her people would come and fill her bowl; these were, quite simply, the greatest days of her life. The cool, clear water flowed from the garden hose into her dirty bowl, bubbling and spilling over the worn metal edges, turning the gray, dusty ground around it into a dark stain. She rushed forward to lap at the water coming from the hose, like the tentacle of some life-giving fountain.

The summer days were hard for the little white dog, but she would never trade them for the freezing, dark winter. The height of winter was especially cruel; the thin, plywood walls of her tattered house offered no insulation from the determined cold. Strong, crisp winds blew straight through the large opening that was her door, often dragging snow or ice into her meager shelter. She had the same ritual every night: she would curl herself tightly into the corner, place her head under her front legs and shiver. It seemed that the shivering would never end as the clear, cold nights crept onwards, the hands of time frozen with the rest of the world. For days and nights, she would shiver. Some days, the sun would rise and cast a faint glow of heat on her house. She would leave her corner and walk to the front of her tiny house, dragging her short, rusted chain behind her, and she would stand in the sun, basking in the smallest rays of warmth. In the dead of winter, small moments such as these mattered immensely, and each faint and fleeting ray of sun bore the false hope of better days ahead.

When the snow fell outside, the floor of her house grew bitter cold and her huddling corner proved far less hospitable. The icy chill of the long, dead season permeated through her paws, and the cold drafts and frozen ground beneath her house made the splintered floor uncomfortable. On those cold days, there wasn't even a false hope to cling to. She often stood and paced in her house until she was too tired, and finally her worn body curled apathetically on the cold floor, succumbing to the bleak and icy night.

On very rare occasions, her people would bring

her things — a meager attempt to offer some respite from the cold sometimes a towel, or a blanket, or on one occasion, a tattered piece of carpet. As they stuck their heads in to adjust the item around, they would offer a few kind words, and just like that, they were gone. When the blanket was fresh and new, she quite enjoyed it. She would use her front paws to pull it to her corner, digging her head under part of it and resting her body on top of the rest, her nose twitching at the lingering scent of her people. Sometimes she would ruffle the blanket and toss her head up wildly, trying vainly to spur a game with herself. The game always ended quickly though, as there was no one there to play with. Her new blanket provided some semblance of warmth for a day or so, but she quickly learned that her blanket drew the cold and moisture and eventually became wet, hard, and then frozen. Her house grew even colder as the stiff blanket chilled her pitiful abode from the inside. She would try and push the blanket from her house, but often it would stick in corners, caught on a nail or simply frozen to the hard wood. Her brief joy at the new blanket would soon become misery as she lay on the now frozen covering, the chill of the air even colder against her damp fur.

As much as she dreaded the baking heat of summer and the frosty chill of winter, the little white dog longed for spring and fall.

Even the hottest spring days weren't so bad since she had borne the brunt of the brutal summer and knew she could make it through what was to come. She relished in the gentle, cool breezes that blew across the backyard, rustling the new leaves above and bringing scents from afar. When the grass started to grow, she had a place outside of her house that she could get to, just at the end of her chain; it was a soft spot in the leafy blades where she could sit at the edge of a bed of emerald grass. Sometimes she would roll over and over, feeling the gentle blades across her dirty fur. The soft tingle of a thousand tall blades of grass across her back was heavenly. She couldn't quite reach the whole patch of grass as her chain ended just a few feet into the lush carpet, but these few, precious feet of verdant paradise, the quiet chirping of tiny starlings in the trees, the occasional soft breeze that blew the dust from her short hair, and the distant barks of neighbor dogs suddenly free to enjoy their yards after a long winter, made her heart smile and forget for a while.

Fall brought its own special treats. After the warm summer, she would welcome the cool breeze that pierced the stifling heat and pushed the harsh rays of sun back into the sky. The crisp leaves from the tall oak tree fell all around her patch of dirt, on top of her house, and coated the nearest edge of grass. The leaves seemed to dance as they dropped from the sky, floating softly, twisting and tipping as they cascaded downwards like some autumn curtain. She would jump at them and try to snatch them with her teeth, often pawing at them as they landed and sometimes rolling in small piles of them. In her mind, the leaves were as close to friends as she knew. They fell and danced with her. They played and rolled, each one unique in its shape, smell, and the sound it made as it crackled under her paws.

But as she sat in her doghouse in the stagnant depths of summer, the other seasons felt so far and distant. Today was hot; she longed for the fall, for the cool, crisp air to soften her dried skin and rejuvenate her. She had many hard months ahead before the new season came to refresh her tired spirit. The summer had just begun, and she needed to focus on getting through these long, tedious days. This year would be different than the others, though. She had more than just herself to worry about now.

She glanced down her nose at the jiggling mass of puppies at her belly. There were five of them, each fighting the other for a place at the nipple. She had been nursing like this for days now and had grown very weary, the puppies seemingly relentless in their constant struggle for milk.

In her motherly heart, she could sense their weakness. They were not as strong as they should be, and she felt guilty for it. Her body was spent and tired, and she just wasn't producing enough milk for all of them. Several days ago, one of them had died. The tiny white puppy with black spots had simply stopped moving, stopped squirming, and abruptly stopped her relentless pursuit of milk. Her frail little body lay there in the doghouse for a day and a half before the people came and found her. She had nosed the pathetically small corpse into a corner so that she could keep nursing the others and try to save them. Her heart ached as she sat there for that day and a half with the body of her puppy beside her in the doghouse, knowing that she had failed to keep it alive. The weariness in her eyes was a surprising reprieve — the depths of fatigue and a pair of sagging eyelids kept her from looking at the intrepid flies that gathered on the lifeless pup in the corner of the filthy wooden house.

She hadn't seen the pups' father since the one and only night he came into her yard for a visit. A week before he had come, she had seen the old black Labrador Retriever running through the neighbor's yard at a gallop. He had looked at her through the rusted diamond-shaped holes of the chain-link fence briefly and paused, then kept running. Sadness came over her; her mood had swelled when she first saw him, but the feeling quickly faded as he loafed off through the neighborhood. She felt that she wasn't even worth a second look from the old dog. His brief visit made her long for a friend even more, someone beyond the fall leaves. She wanted companionship, someone to break up the tedious days. Would he come back now that he knew she was there? Would he give her a second look? Would he at least bark at her from across the fence so that she could bark back?

The next day she spotted him again, and her heart rose. He came running slowly through the neighbor's yard one afternoon, looking in her direction the whole time. She stood tall in front of her doghouse, her ears up and her tail wagging slowly back and forth. Her chain pulled as far as it would go. Her body was suddenly full of energy, sending clear signals that she wanted to play. The old black Lab gave a yip and scratched his feet in the grass on the other side of the fence. She yipped back, bending her front legs and sticking her butt in the air with a rapid wiggle of her wiry tail. Before she knew it, the old Lab was over the fence in one smooth motion, his legs nimbler than she had imagined. For once in her life, there was another dog in the yard with her, a friend and companion. For only a short while that day, she forgot about the chain, the unreachable tree, the unrelenting sun. And then before she knew it, the old black Lab was gone. He hadn't been back since.

And so the days went by after his visit, one after the other, each one the same as the last. Then came the puppies. Her people brought her water a little more frequently than they did before, and they brought more food as well, often mixing the hard, dry kibble with water for the puppies as they grew. She ate very little of the sparse offerings, saving every morsel she could for her hungry litter.

The miserable days and weeks passed one into the other, and the puppies grew bigger and bigger, often roaming from the doghouse into the yard. She went as far as she could on her chain to bring them back, but sometimes they just wandered to the edge of the yard, peering through the low chain-link fence that kept them confined. They always came back to mother, though, and that brought her a precious ounce of joy.

# CHASING THE BLUE SKY

The little puppies gave her life, their exuberance and vigor untainted by hundreds of days of cold and heat at the end of a wretched chain.

There were only four puppies now; a few weeks back, one more had passed silently in the night. She was grateful that her people had found this one more quickly than the last, coming in the morning to take its body away. She mourned the death of her second pup although the remaining four seemed not even to notice the passing of their sibling. There was little time for sadness, though. She had a hungry family to tend to, and if they were to stay together and alive, all of her thoughts would need to be on the young dogs growing rapidly around her.

Her puppies were a handsome litter of mixed colors; there was a white girl with brown and black spots, a brown girl with white boots, a solid white boy, and a black boy with streaks of white on his nose and chest. They grew quickly into a little pack, generally obeying their mother and forming the beginnings of a cohesive little family. The puppies happily played around the yard but stayed mostly near the doghouse, longing for the comfort of their mother. Over time, each began to develop their own personality. The girls, in general, were bossy, often pushing the two boys into the corner of the doghouse or romping on top of them in the yard. The little white boy seemed to play well, enjoying the frolicking with his sisters. The black dog, however, was quieter. He enjoyed his time with his mother, and he rarely left her side. She appreciated how much he remained with her.

These were happy days for her; the time with her pack invigorated her and brought her purpose beyond the physical limitations of the backyard. When she was with her puppies, she could forget — ever so briefly — the lonely days she shared with only the sun and cold. She came to love her little family and settled naturally into the role of doting mother. Though she had lost two of her children, she comforted herself with how much the others had grown and developed. Each morning she would look forward to the day ahead with her lively little brood.

But things changed one day. People started to come into the backyard — strange people, different people. As the days went past, many new faces with their strange smells and staring eyes had entered her yard, all uncomfortably focused on her tiny corner of the world. The man was always with them though, so she believed that everything would be alright.

She could always tell when people were coming. Just before they would come, the man always brought her fresh water and food, and sometimes he even swept out her doghouse. She liked it when the man cleaned out the doghouse. Sometimes it would get dusty and stale with a thick layer of crust forming on the floor. The bodies of bugs would often clog the corners and crunch under her filthy paws.

When the first set of strange people came, she was scared. She gave a few yips to warn this new man and woman to stay away from her puppies. The puppies didn't listen, and they ran through the yard towards the newcomers. She felt helpless as she tugged on her chain, calling with futility for her puppies to come back to her. Her man calmed her down and talked to her in a soft voice, coming to pet her for the first time in a long time. It was a rare treat that he did this, but she gave in to his uncharacteristically soft voice and began to calm down. She trusted the man — maybe these new people weren't so bad.

The new people were there for only a short while, standing in the yard, talking with the man, and laughing as her puppies rolled and tumbled in the grass as they enjoyed the attention. The new people pointed several times. They must be admiring how handsome her puppies were, she thought. After a bit, the strange, new woman picked up the white boy and held him in her arms. The little white dog was worried at first — she pulled on her chain and whined, trying to get to her pup. The man comforted her again with a few words, and she closely watched the woman gently holding the pup. *It will be alright*, she thought, *the man is here, and I can trust him.* The new people talked some more and laughed a little, and everything seemed to be alright for the moment. Her pup was doing fine, enjoying the attention of the woman. She watched as the two men exchanged something and then shook hands. She whined again for her pup, but suddenly, the two men and the woman turned and walked away, still holding her puppy. She whined louder this time, thinking that maybe they hadn't heard her. Her sharp bark punctuated the end of a long howl. She whined at their backs as they left the yard through the front gate with her puppy, but they never turned around. She barked and whimpered at the end of her short chain, but no one listened.

And so it had gone for many days now: various people had come to her yard and gawked at her puppies. Each time she was scared, but the man would comfort her and tell her it was okay. She wanted to believe him each time but could not help the worry from creeping into her heart, for each time these strange people came they left with another one of her puppies until there was only one. Her heart had broken three times now. Her little world, her brief respite of happiness was being chipped away one puppy at a time. She lay in front of her doghouse, her chin resting lifelessly in the dirt, her eyelids heavy and low over her eyes. Her spirit, briefly renewed by the life of her pack, was broken once more.

The little black pup wriggled his nose into his mother's side, pushing her and trying to revive her spirits. Even in the ignorance of his youth, he could sense the sorrow in her. His nose rubbed the dirt as he pushed at her again, then he jumped up and sneezed the tickling dirt from his nostrils, shaking his head like the tiniest clown. He landed on all fours and crouched low, giving a comical yip at his mother. She did not respond and instead just lay there, eyes staring off into nothing. Wish as she might, she could not bring herself to stir or play with him.

# CHASING THE BLUE SKY

The black pup would not be deterred by her indifference; he would play by himself if his mother would not join in. He ran hard towards a tall patch of grass just outside the reach of his mother's chain and tumbled sideways, the long blades caressing his soft fur, then sprang to his feet and attacked the grass that had caused his roll. The white dog cast a sideways glance at her playful puppy. *His spirit is good*, she thought. She admired the liveliness of the little dog. His brothers and sisters had all gone before him, taken away by the strange people, yet this little dog had stayed by his mother's side, keeping her company during the hot days and always trying to cheer her when she was down. He was a good puppy indeed, and she was glad he was with her. She knew not what had happened to the rest of her litter, and it scared her to think of them alone outside the yard, but she had gradually moved past those thoughts and had focused on all she had left — this loyal, black puppy with the white streak up his nose. It had been a week since her three puppies had been taken from her. One week the two of them had been alone in the yard. They had formed a routine and he listened to her well, staying close to her side. She treasured the nights they slept together in the doghouse. She would curl into a ball as the puppy nestled into the warmth of her curled body. The sadness of losing her other puppies would never leave her, but this little black puppy did much to fill the void.

And then one typical, hot summer day, no different than the rest, she heard the handle turn on the back door. She rose with eager anticipation — perhaps a visit from her person meant a bowl of cool water or some food, she wondered. The door opened slowly, and the man stepped out followed by a great many people. There was another new man accompanied by a woman, and this time two children, a boy and a girl. She could sense their excitement. The two children spoke excitedly, their small hands covering their mouths. It made her happy just hearing them. Her man walked down the steps, leading the group to the dog-house. She no longer yipped when people came to her house; she had learned that it did no good, and no one listened anyway.

Behind her, the little black pup rustled from the doghouse and started towards the group, his fat belly, full of worms, hanging low to the ground. The children bent down, and he waddled to them instinctively as they cooed and made soft noises to him. She stood at the edge of her dirt, her heart slowly growing heavy, her tail wagging slowly... pensively. She scanned these new people in her yard, looking at their expressions. They were all looking at her pup, smiles creasing their faces except for her man who stood stoically, speaking some words slowly to the new man. As she looked at them, the woman looked up from the puppy and stared right into her dark yellow eyes. The little white dog stared back, her eyes lifeless and flat, her mouth slightly open, panting hesitantly against the heat. She thought she noticed a brief flash of sadness on the woman's face, but then the woman turned away purposefully, her gaze going back to the puppy. A slow smile once again lined the woman's face as she watched the black puppy dance around the children's feet.

The children picked up the puppy, the little boy holding it to his chest while the girl stroked its floppy ears. The men talked once more, the new man reaching into his pocket for something and handing it to her man, and they shook hands. Then the group turned to leave, the little boy lifting the black puppy higher in his arms so that its head rested on his shoulder.

Across the soft grass they walked, the two men, the woman, the children... and the black puppy — her last puppy.

She knew. As she watched, her spirit died a fourth and final time. The world became silent, and the soft breeze seemed to settle into an unearthly stillness. She stared at the group as they opened the gate. The squeak of the rusty latch was but a faint and distant sound in the deadness of her emotions. Her heart sank, and a deep sadness overcame her like nothing she had experienced before.

In the distance, she watched them leave the yard, one by one: first the men, and then the children, and the woman last. As the boy passed through the gate, she could barely make out the face of her puppy with his head hanging off the boy's shoulder. She was sure she heard him cry with two quick yips across the yard. He was scared, and she was helpless.

As the woman turned to pull the gate closed behind her, she cast one last look at the little white dog. Even from this distance, she could see a deep frown on the woman's face.

Her mouth moved silently as she looked back into the yard towards the doghouse. "I'm sorry," she said to the little white dog.

Then the woman looked down, pulled the gate closed, and dropped the latch. She turned her back and left, the whole family fading into the distance, the black puppy with them — forever gone.

The little white dog sat there for a long, long time watching the fence, waiting and hoping that someone would return. But they never did. As the sun began to set and the lights of neighboring houses flickered on in the distance, she pushed her legs forward slowly in the dirt until she was laying down. She rested her head on her front legs. Her eyes drooped with sadness, and she let out a deep, sorrowful sigh.

High above her, perched watchfully on the bough of the old oak, sat the small, brown squirrel. His nose twitched as he gazed down through eyes of black onyx at the figure below him, tragically caught somewhere in the cruel middle-ground of man where the tame creatures lived — obedient, yet still enslaved. As the defeated white dog sank into the dirt, the squirrel climbed higher into the tree, untamed, unchained, and free.

# CHAPTER 2

The lilting, gentle voice of a small child woke the black puppy from his deep slumber. His nose brushed softly against the warm threads of a plush blanket as he lifted his weary head to greet the noise. He stretched his spindly legs in front of him and arched his tiny back, lifting his head skyward in a long, deep stretch. The sounds of the little girl laughing merrily at his efforts to wake echoed like happy music in his floppy ears. He felt safe and protected without a care in the world.

Although it had only been a few days since he left his mother in the backyard, in the blank canvas of a puppy's mind, it seemed an eternity. The blistering heat of the doghouse floor on his unworn paws seemed so distant now, so far removed from this new world of blankets, moist food, cool air from the slatted vents, the constant interest of curious children, and the toys laid at the edge of his colorful, plush bed. There were so many toys that some days his biggest worry was choosing which one to play with. Today might be the fluffy, purple dinosaur that squeaked if chewed in just the right place. Tomorrow might be the rubber ball with the knobby bumps that soothed his small teeth, or perhaps the brightly colored rope that he tugged so ferociously with the children.

Occasionally, he would think about his mother and wonder where she was and what she must be thinking. He thought that she must surely be in a home by now, somewhere indoors far away from the blistering sun. His brother and sisters had gone before him, and he just knew they had found homes too. Surely after he left some other new people must have come to the yard, shaken hands with the man, and taken his mother away — out of the yard, off of the chain, and away from her old, sad doghouse. He envisioned his mother and siblings, resting their tired, happy heads on warm blankets just like his with colorful toys of their own. He was too young to think much beyond that, but in the rare moments when the children and the house were quiet, and he lay alone in his bed, his young mind wandered to these thoughts. He just couldn't imagine it any other way.

"Good morning, Tobbbbyyy," said the girl, stringing the words together in a playful melody as she peered down at the little puppy, a bright white smile creased beneath a pair of deep, emerald eyes.

Toby finished his stretching and flopped on his side dramatically, looking up at the young girl. The dancing stray wisps of her brown hair mesmerized him as his small eyes tracked their movement. She reached down gently and began to rub his rounded chest with a tiny, bony hand. Toby's body arched in delight as he savored the soft scratch of her fingernails across the length of his body.

"Do you want to go outside and *potty*?" she asked him, the last word hanging in the air, carefully and purposefully emphasized.

*Poddy*, thought Toby. He knew that word now. The little girl said it every time before he went outside. "Poddy" meant to go outside, to drain his tiny bladder. He always felt so good after he peed, and he knew it made his people happy as they often cheered and sometimes clapped. *Yes, I want to poddy*, thought Toby as he rustled in his bed.

The little girl lifted him gently and held him against her arms, his nose ingesting a thousand scents from her soft hair. He felt safe in her arms and thought that he would like to stay there forever, but he really had to poddy. As she walked towards the rear of the house, Toby could see his kingdom: the large leather sofas where he sat with the children, the curious box that flashed pictures and made strange sounds, the tall wooden table where the family gathered to eat. *What a place*, he thought.

"Go potty!" said the girl cheerfully, swinging the door open with one hand as she cradled Toby with the other. The warm sun shone down on his thin black fur, subtle and welcoming, so different than the aggressive sun he previously knew.

The little girl set him down at the base of the steps and took a few paces backward, watching him with precious intrigue. Toby craned his neck to look up at the girl, but the sun's rays were shining in his eyes, making him squint and blink. The little girl laughed at his twitching face. After a moment, he turned his head and waddled unsteadily down the short, wooden stairs into the soft grass of the yard.

His little legs steered him towards the closest patch of grass. The blades tickled his belly as he walked out a few paces then he squatted his hind legs and began to pee. Before he finished, he heard a second voice behind him — the voice of the young boy.

"Tobyyyyyyy!" he shouted, a familiar childish glee accompanying his name. The boy, a few years younger than his sister, had the same fair skin and sandy hair. He bounded down the stairs and into the yard towards Toby just as he finished his morning business.

As the boy approached, Toby made a short charge towards him and rose awkwardly on his rear two legs, flailing his paws forward at the boy in a sign of play. Then just as quickly, he dropped into a crouch, and as the boy approached, Toby tried to dart to his left. His uneasy legs foiled his endeavor though, and he stumbled and fell to the grass in a furry heap. The little boy was soon in the grass with him, rolling him from side to side and scratching his muzzle as he made gentle, unintelligible cooing sounds that carried across the yard on the warm summer breeze.

And so it was for Toby in his early days as a puppy with the family. Life was so much better than before. One day turned into two, and two into a week, and before long, Toby became a cherished companion in the household. His bed was always clean and fluffed, his meals were always prompt and full, and his room was filled with so many toys. And there was certainly no shortage of love for the little black dog.

As the days and weeks passed, Toby bonded with the family. The man he came to know as Peter would wake early each morning and pick up Toby's bright blue nylon leash for a walk. The jingling of the metal clasp sent eager anticipation through the young dog as he quickly understood the meaning behind the curious sound. Toby and Peter developed a special relationship on their walks. Peter would let Toby stop and sniff and even chase the foraging birds and chipmunks to the end of the leash with nary a harsh word. Toby often looked longingly at him, admiring this new companion and protector. Peter was tall and sturdy. He had wavy brown hair and friendly eyes accompanied by a perpetual smile. Rarely did Toby feel safer than when he was with Peter on their walks or runs.

The woman was called Sandra. She was kind to Toby as well, though he always sensed some feelings within her that he could never quite place. He thought he felt some sorrow or guilt whenever she held him, but he was never quite sure. She was not as open with her emotions as the man or even the children were. She would talk to Toby gently, and at times he could see the sadness in her light blue eyes. For a long while, Toby believed her emotions were over something he had done, but he came to understand that it was deeper than that — it was something distant and untouchable. But he loved her just the same.

When Toby turned 6-months-old, the family began to put him in the car the same night each week and take him far from the house to a small brick building surrounded by fields and fences. Usually one of the children would come and find him and in an excited voice say, "Toby, are you ready for *class*?" Then the whole lot of them would pack into the big car and drive off to this strange building, chattering happily along the way.

The trainer was a slim, young woman named Becky. Her hair was curly but always pulled back into a ponytail, and her blue shirt was always crisp and fresh, tucked in just right to her khaki pants. Becky was friendly but firm; her soft voice carried sounds both high and low, and Toby instinctively knew what she meant on many occasions just from the tone of her voice. The family was so proud of him as he learned his basic commands. There were "sit" and "stay" and "come" and "heel." Toby wasn't the greatest with his stay as he sometimes grew bored and longed to do something more interesting, but he would sit or lay down for a treat without a moment of hesitation. Sometimes when they asked him to sit, he would sit and stand and then sit again, hoping for an extra treat. This ploy rarely worked, although occasionally the family would smile and reward him for his ruse.

The training classes were Toby's first real experience with other dogs outside of the short time he spent with his mother and siblings in the backyard. Occasionally when out on a run with Peter, another dog would pass quickly, but he never got a chance to sniff and romp with them. Class was different though. And before each class started, there always seemed to be time to run and play on the hard rubber surface of the classroom floor.

Toby's class was full of all sorts of dogs. Each one had their own personality, quirks, mannerisms, smells, and sounds. The diversity of Toby's classmates gave him a well-rounded introduction to what it truly meant to be a dog.

First, there was the rotund, furry white terrier named Duke. He was quite portly and proud to say the least. While his name was Duke, he was most certainly the king of the class — parading around, barking at his classmates in his high-pitched yip, lifting his jaw in a dignified fashion towards the ceiling with each bark, and his fluffy belly hanging just an inch or so off the ground.

Then there was Bella, a medium-sized black dog of sleek coat and long limbs. Bella was a shy dog; she was sweet, quiet, and always close to her owner. She seemed almost afraid of the other dogs in the class. Her parents were very patient with her, recognizing the shyness of her demeanor. They talked in slow, soothing voices and always praised her with scratches and rubs whenever she did the slightest thing.

Next, there was Frankie, a shaggy, long-haired mutt of a dog with patches of tan and white flowing from his coat in measured patterns. He was a younger dog, maybe just a few years older than Toby. He was well-tempered and even-keeled, clearly the apple of his human family's eye. Frankie always seemed to know what the trainer was going to ask next and was savvy well beyond his years.

Then there was Luigi, the smallest dog in the class. He weighed only a few pounds, and his buggish eyes peered out over a pointed snout. He made up for his small stature with an abundance of character. Toby didn't much care for Luigi because he was always interrupting and making noise when the teacher was talking, trying to get everyone to look at him. Luigi's dad, a smallish, older man with a pot belly and funny hat, always looked so embarrassed at his antics, but he seemed at a loss as to what to do.

Lastly, there was Emma, who appeared to be a mix of everything under the sun. Toby thought that perhaps she was some type of athletic breed mixed with some hound. She was friendly enough, but very high energy and could never seem to stay focused on the lessons. Toby could sense the energy pulsating from her. She was always anxious, on alert, ready to move and run. Her energy distracted Toby and often caused him to lose focus on the teacher.

Of all the dogs in class, Toby by far enjoyed his interactions with Frankie the most. Seeing how the pair hit it off, the families of the two dogs began to arrive to class early just to give the two dogs some time to romp and play around the training room. They zipped and pranced and rolled and dove. Toby didn't realize it at the time, but Frankie was teaching Toby cues, signals, and how to read another dog. Frankie was so calm and good-natured, and their play sessions taught young Toby far more than a human ever could.

Toby didn't know what it meant, but the humans said Frankie was "adopted." They said something about him having been in a place called a "shelter" before he came to live with them. None of it made sense to Toby, but Frankie's parents spoke proudly of it, their tones always so serious when they told the story. Toby didn't care where Frankie came from; he was a good dog and a good friend, and that was just fine with Toby.

Every time the pair met before class, Frankie was calm and friendly, never overeager despite their week apart. Frankie always greeted Toby with a gentle nudge of his muzzle to let him know he remembered and was glad to see him again. The families enjoyed watching their interactions, dropping the leashes and standing back, looking on as young Toby tried to keep up with the older dog, charging at him, jumping to put his paws on Frankie's back and then rolling over in a submissive pose when the Frankie would spin and nudge him to the ground. The children were especially tickled watching their young dog learn the ways of doghood from the older, wiser dog.

Over their time in class together, Toby learned a great deal from Frankie. He learned what play was too rough and what was just right. He learned how to chase and how to greet another dog. He learned how to turn corners quickly on the run. But most of all, he learned what it was like to have his first real friend. Frankie was a true friend, indeed, something he had not known since he left his brothers, sisters, and mother many months ago in that far-away backyard.

Although Toby knew nothing of it, despite his outward calm, Frankie's short life had been turbulent. The shaggy dog's sad history brewed just below the surface under his confident persona. As his earliest recollection, Frankie could vaguely remember being a bundle of warmth in the arms of a woman. He remembered being just a tiny puppy, being cradled and cared for. He remembered his very first home with people that doted on him and cared for him. He remembered toys and treats and playing with the neighbor's dog as he grew older.

Then all at once, things changed for Frankie, and he remembered that day as well. One morning, Frankie's humans bundled up his bed and toys and took him for a car ride. He could feel the mood of his family around him and was unaccustomed to the unspoken tension and nervousness that permeated the car. *This isn't a family trip to the park to play ball,* he thought. He shivered in the back seat as the silence in the car sank into him, the solemn mood of the family creeping into his heart. His whiskers trembled up and down his long snout. No laughing or happy talk. No children talking in high pitches. Nothing but cold, raw silence.

# CHASING THE BLUE SKY

Frankie remembered the car parking in a strange lot. The doors opened, and the man walked around, took Frankie's leash and pulled him from the car. Frankie could remember the foreboding concrete building ahead of him, the terrifying walk to the door of this foreign place. He remembered pressing all four feet into the ground to brace himself as the rusted door squeaked open on its great hinges, bellowing forth loud noises and awful smells that filled his nostrils with pungent fear.

Frankie wanted nothing more than to run back to the car, back to his people. But the man pulled him onwards through the door. He had no idea where he was, but the scents of feces, urine, and musky fur rushing at his sensitive nose embodied the turmoil he knew lay beyond those doors. Frankie stopped dead in his tracks and lay on the ground, unwilling to move farther. The man tugged at him again, but he fought and scratched at the slick floor of the lobby. His memories ran together after that. His young mind simply could not absorb everything that day. There were people looking at him, poking him with needles, touching him all over. There were the sounds of barking and the yelping of dogs in pain. That day and those few that followed were quite simply the worst days of Frankie's life.

But before too long, the darkness began to fade. After a short time in the noisy shelter, a nice, plump, older lady with wiry, white hair and thick red glasses started coming to visit him. At first, she would only pass him and smile, moving on to some other dogs after a moment, but always asking the kennel attendant a few questions about Frankie. After a few days of this, she came back two days in a row, and it was clear that Frankie was the reason for her visit. She would take him out for walks, talking to him in the play yard and watching carefully as he interacted with several other dogs. After that second day, he was free. The noises and smells of the shelter fell far behind him as he looked out the rearview window of the older woman's car while they pulled away from the horrible building.

Then before long, he was in the woman's home, meeting her three dogs, laying by her fireplace and having his own crate with a soft bed to lay in. His affection for the woman grew quickly, and she clearly felt the same about him. But he could tell that she was not letting herself get too attached to him. She would work with him on commands and take him on walks and to lots of places, but there was always some barrier there, a wall that Frankie could never crack. He never felt that he truly touched her heart.

And before he knew it, Frankie was off to another home, laying on another floor with another family. He wasn't sure how it happened. Some people came to visit one day, and the friendly, plump lady with her tall socks and sandals and her funny red glasses took him out back to meet them. The strangers seemed nice enough, and the humans talked pleasantly together. Then the older woman gave Frankie a kiss on the head, told him to be a "good boy," and watched him leave with the new family. Frankie was nervous at first in his new home and missed the kind words of the lady, but he quickly realized that this place wasn't so bad after all. There was a man and a woman, two small girls, and even another dog in the new family, a young white dog named Ellie with curly, silken white fur and a rather regal bearing.

Frankie sometimes felt that Ellie could be a bit of a snoot, but in the end, he liked his new home quite well. The family cared for him, fed him food that filled his belly, and gave him lots of love, plenty of walks, and another soft bed to sleep in. And Frankie quickly noticed that the wall he felt from the older woman in the red glasses was not there with this new family. This new family loved him with all of their hearts, holding nothing back and spoiling the little dog with everything they had. Frankie knew that he had finally found his home.

But Frankie tried his best to live in the present, and this was all the past. He was here now in this training class, romping and playing with his new friend, Toby. He didn't know Toby's background but hoped his life had been better and that he would never experience the same path. Toby had a family, and they seemed quite good to him. To Frankie, they seemed to be a family who would keep Toby forever.

And so it was for Frankie and Toby. The two young dogs, each from humble beginnings, had happily crossed paths in the present. For the eight weeks of class, they cherished their before-class play time and even occasionally, time after class bounding across the big training hall floor. By the end of those eight weeks, the two dogs had grown to be fast friends.

Back at home, Toby was still the apple of his family's eye. He couldn't have asked for anything more from this world. Some days he was given so many treats of so many different kinds that he didn't know what to do. Duck feet and bacon strips and peanut butter cookies — all of them filled his eager belly. It was good that the family walked him as much as they did, Toby thought, or he'd be a chunky dog like fat, old Duke. Toby lived for his walks. He went on one in the morning and one in the evening. Although the morning walk was shorter, Toby grew fond of this time with Sandra who walked him briskly before her morning shower. She seemed to enjoy the walks as well, fawning attention on the young dog. He could feel the tangible bond growing between the two. Sandra had a soft smile and eyes that filled with emotion, and it was easy for Toby to tell when she was happy or sad. He tried his best to comfort her when she needed it.

For Toby, life was good. He longed for nothing. He had a home, a family, a school, and now a new best friend, Frankie, who he met for regular play dates in the park even long after the obedience class had ended. As Toby's young mind filled with memories of his own, the thoughts of the backyard from where he came receded further and further into the recesses of his memory.

# CHAPTER 3

The seasons came and went for Toby in his new home. As a puppy, he had felt only the torrid summer, so these new times of year each brought their own curious experiences.

Toby learned quite quickly that he wasn't fond of the winter. The snow seeped between his paws and chilled the soft webbing underneath. The ground was either frozen solid or soft and mushy from a sun's thaw, and there seemed to be no comfortable middle ground. Wherever he walked, his paws picked up the snow or dirt that clung in between the grooves of his toes. He would spend a long time after each walk working his tongue deep into the ridges of his paws to clear the clinging debris. Toby quickly learned that dirty feet led to painful feet. In the winter, his pads would grow raw and cracked, and sometimes walking on them hurt if he didn't clean them well.

He had to admit, though, the winter brought some special joys. Toby relished playing in a fresh snow, craning his neck as he ran to watch his tracks form behind him and flinging soft snow with his nose on to the children. The first time Toby saw snow, he was both awestruck and energized. There was a brief tip-toe into the powdery field to make sure it was safe, but that was quickly followed by a maniacal spin around the backyard, the children and even Sandra laughing at him as he ran in circles, his hind legs almost crossing his front legs as his young, powerful limbs propelled him forth.

As winter faded to spring, Toby absorbed himself in the new smells and sounds of the backyard. His walks had become a bit less frequent than they had been before, but he passed the time just as well in his own yard sniffing around the colorful flowers that bloomed and taking in the scents of the woodland creatures. He missed walking with Sandra, but there was a world to explore just outside the house, and he quickly adjusted to his changing routine. The squirrels were a special pleasure to Toby. They would stand and watch him, or at least he thought they were, yet they never seemed to face him. Their beady eyes appeared to be looking at nothing in particular but seeing everything at the same time. Toby never successfully caught a squirrel, but it was not for lack of effort. On a great many occasions, he would pounce and give chase with all of his vigor. As the days passed and Toby became wiser from the many missed chases, he learned how to leverage his body around the turns, and he became more graceful as he zigged and zagged across the yard in pursuit of the furry brown scourges. He was quickly growing comfortable in his adult body, and the backyard creatures of the woods quickly learned to watch out, for Toby the Hunter was on the prowl.

In a way, it was good that he had the woodland creatures to keep him company, as the children had begun to spend their time on other things, seeming to have lost some interest in him as he grew older. Toby was sad at first because he thought he had done something wrong and could not understand why the boy and the girl took less of an interest in him. He tried harder to please them, bringing them toys and setting them at their feet, his soulful eyes asking them to play.

Of the two children, the little boy still showed some interest in Toby. His rosy cheeks always filled with delight when Toby would bring a toy. He never failed to give Toby a firm but friendly pat on the head whenever they passed in the house. The girl had other concerns, though. Their play time in the yard had faded to almost nothing, and Toby missed playing fetch with the little girl who had once looked at him so longingly and used to throw the ball over and over and over again until Toby lay exhausted at the base of the stairs. Toby wasn't quite sure what had happened. Was it because of the time he chewed up her toy purse? Did he not fetch well enough anymore? He couldn't wrap his mind around what had caused it, but he was still happy in his home nonetheless. It was surely better than the scary place that Frankie had told him about with the barking dogs and the horrible smells. And it was certainly better than the backyard he had once called home.

He hadn't seen Frankie in about a month, though. Their last play date was just a short session at the park on the way across town for Peter to run some errands. Toby and Frankie felt rushed in their visit, and they weren't able to fully stretch their legs and exhaust themselves as they had before. Frankie had a look of sadness in his eye when Toby had left that time, almost like he knew he may never see his friend again. It hadn't dawned on Toby at the time what that look meant, but now he sure hoped Frankie was wrong.

Peter and Sandra seemed busy as well with barely any time for Toby. His regular feeding schedule changed after the winter, and sometimes they would forget to give Toby his morning or evening meal, and his stomach would growl with hunger until they finally remembered. But the little dog never fussed. His people were just busy, and Toby was confident that someday soon they would get back to the old routine.

It was a cool, spring evening, around the time the sun hung low on the horizon, and the porch lights flickered on across the street. Toby had just finished a bowl of hard, dry kibble that he ate hungrily in the corner of the kitchen. The family had gathered at the kitchen table for their meal. Toby paced slowly to his bed in the living room to watch his family eat. He had learned not to beg, so he would often sit and watch instead, hoping one of the children would look up and say his name or throw him a small piece of human food. More often than not, his patience earned him some scraps of food after dinner. The scraps had been less frequent of late, just like everything else, but the boy almost always remembered to bring Toby something when he finished. Sometimes it was just a piece of bread crust, but other times a morsel of meat from the plate.

There was something special about the meal tonight, though. Toby could tell that Peter and Sandra were anxious, exchanging glances with each other, a sort of giddy excitement within them. The little dog scooted towards the edge of his bed, wanting and longing to be a part of the discussion, to be a part of the family at the table. The parents began to speak, and he could feel the energy building in the children. The boy and the girl had set their forks down and were listening intently as Peter spoke a few words more, reaching to the woman to take her hand in his. Toby perked his ears and crooked his head. He was just as eager as the boy and the girl to hear what was about to be said.

"Samantha, Mason," said the man, calling the children by name and looking each of them in the eye as he spoke. "We have some exciting news and we're hoping that you'll be just as happy as we are. Ok, guys?"

The boy and girl scooted forward in their seats in anticipation as Peter lifted Sandra's hand and grasped it closer to him, turning to look at her with a broad, affectionate smile.

Sandra smiled back, her broad lips opening to reveal a beautiful smile, her cheeks glowing in the light of the overhead lamp, and then she spoke. "You're going to have a little brother or sister. Mommy is pregnant."

The cheers rose suddenly from the boy and girl so quickly that Toby was startled and inadvertently jumped back on his cushion at the sharp noise. The children cheered with the boisterous raucousness of innocent delight. The girl, Samantha, was quickly off her chair, running and hugging her mother and father while Mason turned his head to the table and shook it excitedly back and forth, exclaiming "Yesssssss!!!" Peter and Sandra's faces broke into giant smiles as the boy and girl engulfed them both with wild hugs.

After hugging his parents, the boy pushed his chair back from the table and ran towards Toby in the next room, his superhero sneakers pounding hard on the wooden floor. He tucked his legs into a slide and glided to a sharp landing at the edge of Toby's bed. Toby, still bewildered from the eruption of cheers, pulled back, his eyes grew wide as the boy catapulted onto his bed and wrapped his arms around him. "We're gonna have a baby, Toby! You hear that?!? This is awwweeesome!" he shouted, scratching Toby behind the ears as the young dog struggled to digest everything that was going on. The family was clearly happy, maybe even happy with him, or at least the boy was. Had Toby done something good? Was there a treat in it for him? Perhaps a large peanut-buttery bone?

There was no treat that night though. And for many nights more there were no treats as things in the house began to change even more and it seemed that Toby had become all but forgotten after the strange commotion at the dinner table.

Soon the spring faded away and summer came, bringing with it the unbridled heat of the sun. The lingering swelter of those long months made Toby think more and more of his mother. He suddenly longed to be with her again, longed to know that she was happy. He hoped that she had found some respite from the miserable yard and the molded doghouse, the only home his old mother ever knew.

As the slow days of summer passed, Toby found himself spending more and more time in the yard. Sometimes when the family was at work and the kids were at school, they would leave him out there all day long.

"He needs to get used to it," he heard Peter tell Sandra one day. A familiar sadness crossed her face again.

The drudgery of summer wore on Toby. He had no doghouse, only the shade of a large oak tree and a few feet of shadow around midday cast by the long eaves of the house. He found himself laying in the dirt for hours on end, listless and aimless. He grew weary. Sometimes it was too hot to take a nap, so he'd walk the yard, looking for a spot the sun had not touched, looking for the shade and some cool dirt that he rarely found.

His family still brought him in at night though. And in the house, he still had his bed, although it was ragged and torn now. Blemishes of dirt and grass that he carried in from the backyard had stained the bed. He had pulled stuffing from one corner in a fit of boredom one day. *This is still better than the hard ground*, he thought.

Even the toys were fewer. There was no more stuffed octopus or squeaky koala bears. No more rawhides. Occasionally, he would still get a tennis ball and a handful of treats that tasted only marginally better than the stuffing from his old dog bed.

"We need to save money for the baby. We'll have to cut back on things," Peter had said to Sandra one day. Toby didn't understand these words. They talked a lot, often in very serious and worried tones. But Toby couldn't understand.

As the months passed, things continued in this way. Long days in the yard in the company of the basking sun, lots of time alone with the scant remnants of a worn tennis ball, and a family who now seemed to have all but forgotten him. The little dog was sinking into oblivion.

As he always was, though, the little boy remained kind to Toby, his childish exuberance seemingly unaware of the change that had overtaken the others. He would still talk to Toby and play games with him every so often. Once, the boy even spent quite some time working to teach Toby some new tricks. Toby was already well versed in "sit" and "down." This time, the boy taught him how to shake as he raised his paw over and over again and placed it gently in the boy's tiny hand. Maybe if he could master this "shake," Toby could work his way back into their hearts. So try and try he did, shaking left and shaking right whenever the boy showed his hand. It only took a matter of minutes before Toby was following the boy's every command to the delight of the young child.

"Daddy! Look what Toby can do!" he shouted across the living room one day, as Peter sat at the sofa working feverishly on his laptop. The man glanced up briefly over his glasses, the boy catching his eye to ensure that he was watching. When the boy turned back to Toby and said "shake," the little dog lifted his paw as quickly as he could, hoping the man would see, hoping he would remember all the fun times they had, the walks, the playtime with Frankie, the park…

As Toby's paw landed softly in Mason's open hand, the dog looked towards Peter, seeking a sign of his approval. Peter's head was down, peering back into the bright abyss of his open laptop. Toby's heart sank, and his eyes dropped to the floor. The boy knelt before him, wrapped his arm around the back of his neck and whispered in his big ear. "I still love you," he said.

# CHAPTER 4

T he sluggish days of summer eventually gave way to the brisk winds of a welcome fall. Toby spent much more time in the backyard now, alone with the wandering thoughts of a confused, young dog. On some nights he would not come in at all. Sometimes he would lie still on the hard, unforgiving wood of the back deck, trading the comfort of the grass for the desire to be closer to his people on the other side of the door. His coat had grown dusty and the black had turned to brown. His fur was layered with dirt and layers of loose hair desperate for a good combing. His paws grew calloused and hard, often forming deep cracks on his pads. His nails were long and unkempt, far removed from the gradual filing of the pavement on his long walks or runs.

The worst days were the wet ones, the ones when the skies would open up and unleash torrents of rain through the sparse trees of the backyard. The family had purchased a plastic doghouse for Toby a few months back. Even Toby knew then that this was a foreboding sign of his transition from beloved house dog to backyard ornament.

The house was tall, white, and shaped like an igloo. The stickers plastered to the outside said it was insulated from cold and heat and showed a picture of a happy dog curled comfortably inside. The boy had pressed his father to purchase the nicest home for Toby, and only after such constant badgering did he relent to the expense. On the few nights Toby slept in the igloo, he didn't feel much like the happy dog in the picture. He couldn't imagine what made that dog so happy to be sleeping alone in a hollow, plastic house. He only knew he was lonely here. When the autumn chill came, and the cool winds rushed through the wide-mouthed opening, Toby could only turn his back to the cold and shiver himself to sleep.

Sometimes at night, the sounds of the woodland creatures would rouse him from his slumber. The insects chirped relentlessly, an owl hooted, and branches cracked under the weight of a scavenging raccoon or opossum. Toby would rise from the hard, plastic floor of the igloo, groaning away the sleepiness, and take a few paces outside to investigate. Deep down inside, he hoped he would catch sight of some nocturnal creature in the yard if only to feel the presence of another soul however foreign they may be. But while the rustling noises betrayed their presence, he never saw them.

And so he would sit just outside the lip of his doghouse and think of the creatures that went unseen all around him. They were creatures of their own routines, their nights not for sleeping, but for gathering and hunting. Unlike Toby, who still at least received semi-regular meals, the noises and shapes in the trees could count on nothing. They were independent and free, and while they faced daily pressures of survival, they depended on no one but themselves. These thoughts weighed on Toby and caused him to reflect on his own situation. He would grow even more depressed, contrasting the lives of these creatures with his own dependency on the family and their growing apathy towards him. The thoughts caused an ache in his heart.

Every once in a while, Toby was allowed to come inside the house. These sporadic episodes seemed a nostalgic tribute to days not that long ago when the home was a home for all, dog and human alike. Most of the time Toby was let in the house because the boy incessantly prompted his mother and pleaded with her to let him come in. Mason had a way of being persistent. Very infrequently, Sandra would relent and open the back door for Toby. The boy would step to the yard and call for him, his tone largely unchanged from the jubilance of those early days. Toby didn't need to be called twice and would sprint to the back door, leaving his worries to trail behind him in the yard. Invariably, Sandra would grimace at the sight of the dirty dog, usually taking an old towel and wiping down his coat as he stood patiently in the laundry room.

The simple gesture of allowing Toby to cross the threshold into the house changed his demeanor dramatically. For a moment, he was the Toby of old again, his spirit renewed at his place with the family. His tail wagged feverishly, and his mouth would open into a broad smile, his pink tongue showing behind his still-white teeth. Toby would nuzzle his nose into the back of Sandra's legs, thanking her profusely for this privilege. She always gave the boy a melancholic smile, one that said she wanted to share in the happiness with him, but that it was tainted with the knowledge that it was temporary. Her complicity in Toby's banishment to the backyard was difficult to suppress. But Toby was aware of none of this. In his mind he was exactly where he wanted to be.

For the brief times that Toby was indoors, the boy was his constant companion, leading him from room to room and showing him any changes to the home, new toys, or anything remotely interesting. Toby would follow the little boy intently, his eyes staring wide, listening for commands, tail slapping hard against the drywall of the narrow hallways. The little girl was more aloof but occasionally she would step out of her room and pat Toby on the head and then just as quickly walk away, leaving him panting wide-mouthed for more.

As the days drew deeper into fall, the family drew further away from Toby. The woman's belly grew round and full, and as it grew it seemed to draw all of the attention and compassion in the house. The burgeoning belly and the child inside left little concern for anything else, especially a dirty dog cast to the sequestered backyard.

One particular day late in October as the leaves swirled around the yard from a whipping westerly wind, Toby walked the perimeter of the fence. He sniffed and scratched, looking dolefully for anything new or of interest. Perhaps he might find a chipmunk hole under the fence or a wayward sassafras leaf to occupy his mind. As he made his way around the yard, he came upon one of the back windows of the house and peered in to see what the family was doing this evening. When he was bored and the lights of the house shone bright to let him know that his people were awake, he would occasionally perch in this spot beside the deck and watch. Once or twice before, they had seen him looking in and one of them, often the boy or Sandra, would come to let him in. Whether they wanted him near them or were simply unable to continue their activities with the sad eyes just over the edge of the windowsill was unknown.

But on this evening, no one saw him watching. The family was gathered at the kitchen table. Peter was at the head of the table doing most of the talking. At the far end of the table was Sandra, her head down, thoughtfully and slowly chewing her meal.

Peter talked and talked, sometimes leaning down close to the boy who sat to his right and other times staring straight down at the floor, unable or unwilling to make eye contact with the children. The little girl looked angry, her tiny brow furrowed, her fists clenched, and the bright red of frustration showed through the part in her pigtails.

# CHASING THE BLUE SKY

And suddenly, as if shot from a rocket, the boy stormed from the table, knocking his chair over on the way and charging into the living room in a huff. His shouts and wails vibrated the glass window. Toby looked on, leaning forward on his front legs and letting out a low whimper of concern. He yearned to be closer to his boy.

Sandra looked slack-jawed at Peter, who looked back at her flatly, sighed, and shook his head. Then he pushed his seat back and rose, calmly walking after the little boy in the other room, just out of sight of Toby.

The little girl, still seated at the table, bowed her head and wept. Toby didn't know what was happening in the house, but he didn't like it at all. As Sandra reached across the table to comfort the little girl, Toby stood on his hind legs, clawing at the glass of the back window. Whatever it was, he could help. He could do something if they would just let him in. He clawed and clawed, swiping his long nails across the smooth, slippery glass of the window.

After a moment, Sandra turned to the sounds on the window. Between the darkness and the reflection of the kitchen light, she could make out two eyes, peering into the house, peering deep into her heart. Toby stopped his clawing and stared at her, his eyes pleading something almost spiritual in nature. She bowed her head at the sight, and she, too, began to cry.

That night passed more slowly than any other that Toby could remember. It passed even slower than those humid nights with his mother that he only vaguely remembered, those nights plagued with the smell of rotted wood, the sounds of sick siblings wheezing. Even slower than those early nights alone, when he first was dispatched to the backyard and the flicker of lights inside was his only companion. Those nights when the desolate sense of loneliness clung to every branch of every tree in the yard. This night was somehow different. There was something grave in the air, a thick, solemn murk that hung above the house like a stalled storm cloud. The lights had gone off hours ago. No one had come to check on him before they went to sleep, the shame driving them away from the backyard, away from what they were about to do.

Toby sat by the window of the blackened house for hours. Eventually, he curled into a tight ball and lay down on the old, worn mat by the back door — the one that said, "Wipe Your Paws." After just a few hours of restless sleep, Toby woke to the morning birds with their carefree songs and the soft chill of an autumn breeze. A sense of nervousness clenched his body. Toby didn't know what was happening in the house, but he sensed it was not good. He looked through the window again, hoping for movement and saw none. Taking slow, tentative steps, he walked to the dog-house and tried to find some more sleep. Toby hoped that he would wake to the little boy or even Sandra and all from the night before would be forgotten, passing away as the midnight clouds rolled past the amber moon. Crawling into the doghouse, he twisted his body into the farthest corner of the rounded plastic, closed his eyes, and tried his hardest to fall asleep. But sleep would never come. For two more hours, he laid there, his chin on his paws, his mild jowls hanging awkwardly over his gum line like some sad cartoon character.

With the sun halfway up the morning sky and climbing, the familiar squeak of the back door roused Toby from his dour trance. He jumped to his feet, ducking his head to squeeze through the door, and saw Peter coming down the back steps with the leash in his hand. He raced across the yard, the night's worries fading behind him as he could barely contain his excitement over a long-awaited walk.

Toby charged towards Peter excitedly, stumbling to a halt before him with a half jump, careful to avoid his paws hitting the man. Peter didn't like dirt on his clothes, so Toby flailed his front paws in the air in a desperate attempt to halt his momentum. He succeeded, and Peter gave a half smile and bent down to pat Toby on the head, more of an obligatory pat without any real emotion though. The leash made that long-lost clinking noise as it clamped to Toby's collar and he gave a short pull to let the man know he was all secure and ready for his walk.

Toby clambered up the steps two at a time, his loping gait fueled by the excitement of a morning walk. He did his best to keep from pulling the leash taut and frustrating Peter so soon. Peter guided Toby into the house where he expected to see the rest of the family. The house was silent, still, and lifeless. Toby faltered a moment. The dense quiet came at him suddenly, startling him. His hopes of a walk quickly faded. This was something else.

Walking through the kitchen and down the hallway, Peter, with Toby now hesitantly following behind, turned towards the front door. As they passed through the house, Toby scanned each room for signs of the boy, the girl, or Sandra. But he saw no one. Peter turned the brass knob and led Toby down the front steps, never saying a word. As they reached the bottom of the front steps and turned towards the driveway, Toby saw the car in the driveway with the woman in front, head down as always. The boy and the girl were seated in the rear, their faces shielded by a bright glare from the morning sun. The excitement began to build again. The last time he had ridden with the whole family in the car was for a trip to the park and some play time with Frankie. Could this be happening again?

It took only a second for the sun's reflection to pass the windows and now Toby could see the faces of the children — they were crying. The girl was seated farthest away, head down and crying. The boy's face was pressed against the glass, his eyes stained with the sadness of a thousand tears.

Peter pulled at the leash and guided Toby around to the back of the vehicle. He lifted the gate as he always did when they went for a ride. Toby paused outside momentarily, studied the confusing scene before him and then hopped up into the car. The latch clicked shut behind him. He rushed towards the gate dividing the back space from the rear seats, dragging his leash behind him, and pressed his nose against the bars, smooshing his lips upward on the thin metal bars. The boy turned towards him and placed both hands on the bars, reaching one tiny finger in and scratching Toby on the nose as he continued to cry.

The movement of the car startled Toby, and he braced himself on all fours to avoid falling backward. The noise of the children's sobbing soon merged with the sound of the engine and the road. No one said a word for the longest time, and Toby's anxious mind raced; he was confused and concerned. He licked at the boy's finger, pleading for the boy to give him some sign of what was to come. The boy didn't understand and just kept scratching his nose, his other hand reaching through to pet the dusty fur of Toby's shoulder.

As the road passed before them, Toby grew more and more anxious. He let out a whimper, his eyes grew wide, and he licked feverishly at the boy's fingers. *Tell me something,* he implored in wordless pleas. *Tell me what is happening.*

The boy could sense the dog's anxiety and he began to cry louder. "Daddy! No! We can't do it!" he shuddered, his words staggered through sobs and tears that rolled down his ruddy cheeks.

Peter and Sandra exchanged glances in the front seat, and she turned towards the boy, resting her hand on his shoulder. "Honey, we don't have a choice, I'm so sorry," she said softly. "Your little sister will be here soon, and we just don't have the time for him anymore…" She paused as if letting the words sink in, perhaps trying to convince herself. She looked at Peter for support and continued. "It's not fair to Toby, Mason. He needs to find a new home where they can spend time with him and give him the life he deserves. I'm sorry, sweetie," she said, rubbing his moist cheek with the back of her hand. She turned and looked towards the girl who sat with her head bowed in her own wordless depths of sorrow.

And so the sullen voyage continued on, the children crying and Toby growing more and more anxious at the events around him. Down the highway they went, exiting just near the center of town. The blur of businesses, mechanic shops, sandwich shops, and retail stores whizzed by in the side windows. Peter took a left on a narrow road just past town where the trees were thick and the sky grew narrow through the fall foliage. They traveled down a curvy road for another mile or so, the sound of a couple of vehicles whizzing past the opposite direction the only distraction from the dead, dull loneliness that filled the air. Eventually, the road opened up into a large, gravel parking lot that crunched and bounced under the car's tires.

Toby craned his head to see through the front windshield. Looking through the metal gate and the space between Peter and Sandra, he could just make out the sight of a small, drab, gray building with walls of weathered concrete.

Peter pulled the car slowly and carefully to a stop on the loose gravel just before the gray building. He moved the car to park and turned the key. The sound of the engine faded, and a new sound filled the air: the sounds of countless dogs barking — pained, sorrowful, lonely barking. Toby suddenly grew weak and dizzy, his whole body trembled, his eyes dropped, and he slowly let himself down to lay splayed on the floor of the car. His black fur rippled, and he began to shiver uncontrollably.

# CHAPTER 5

Aside from the boy's muffled sobs and a soft whimpering from the girl, the car had gone quiet, the crunching of gravel and the thrum of the engine giving way to a cold silence. Toby lay hunkered and shivering on the floorboard, unable to see over the seatback that partitioned him from his family. He waited like that for a long moment, hoping one of them would end this whole awful trip with a cheerful "Let's go home!" No one did.

For several long, painful moments they sat wordlessly. The boy's sobbing grew in volume and frequency. Peter and Sandra sat motionless, staring ahead at the concrete blocks that stretched blandly before the car. Neither of them moved to comfort the bawling child.

Finally, Peter's voice broke the silence, the sadness palpable in his broken words. "Guys…I'm sorry," he spoke, the words a mix of sorrow and determination. "He's going to find a better home here, I promise," he continued, the last word sounding hollow in the doleful vacuum of the car.

As the words had barely trickled out of Peter's mouth, the boy shrieked a horrible, pained reply, "He has a home already!"

The boy pounded his little fists into the dull leather of the back seat, causing the car to shudder. There was a long pause and again, the car fell silent. Peter cast a sidelong look at Sandra as if pleading for assistance.

Sandra spoke up, attempting to give hope to her son. "They'll find him a place with other dogs, honey. Somewhere he can live inside and play and be free," she said, her words coming easily, the sadness seemingly vanquished by the image she had conjured. "You know Toby loves to play with other dogs. He'll probably forget us before you know it, Mason," she followed.

The boy did not reply, he only sobbed. Beside him, the girl had tucked her head in her arms and was leaning sideways on the sill of the car window, her small body rising and falling in muted sorrow.

Behind them all, Toby cowered, listening for some inflection or some keywords like "park" or "home" or "treat" or any of the happy words. He heard none.

Taking a deep breath, Peter spoke. "Do you guys want to say goodbye to Toby?" he asked, his voice suddenly taking on a mild sense of exasperation.

Toby looked up at a motion, and suddenly the boy's head was above him, peering through the thin bars of the divider, his eyes luminous in the shimmering moisture of his tears. The boy reached his scrawny fingers through the metal latticework. Toby lifted his head hesitantly and met the small fingers. Though the boy could barely reach him, Toby felt two fingers gently scratch the bridge of his nose, rubbing back and forth against the white streak of fur.

The tears streamed from the boy's eyes, unabated, and he leaned forward and whispered, "I love you forever, Toby." As he spoke, he pressed his lips to the metal. Toby lifted his head some more, leaned forward and pressed his nose against the grate. He could feel the softness of the boy's lips touch his cold, moist nose for only a second, and then the boy was gone, spinning and slumping back to the seat in tears.

"Samantha?" said Sandra.

Toby looked over at the little girl and saw that she sat like a shrunken flower, her arms crossed and her head down, shaking it from side to side defiantly.

"I'm sorry, honey," said Sandra softly.

Toby heard the car door open and Peter step out. In the rear, Toby cowered in the corner, pushing himself forward, closer to the sobbing boy on the other side of the seat.

The rear hatch suddenly opened, and the brightness of the morning sky filled the vehicle with rays of sun. Peter's stood at the rear of the car, casting a long, dark shadow over Toby who lay huddled and shaking in the corner.

"Come on, buddy," Peter said, trying to muster the same voice he used when he and Toby would go for their walks and runs long, long ago. "Let's go for a walk," he said.

CHASING THE BLUE SKY

Toby hunkered deeper into the corner. His faded, black fur rippled in terror and uncertainty. Peter reached in slowly, placing his right hand behind Toby's hips and spinning him in a half circle until he could reach the leash. He took the leash and gave a small tug.

"Come on Toby," he said again, this time more firmly.

Toby felt so conflicted. Simultaneously, he wanted to obey, but he knew better than to leave the car. He started towards Peter and then curled up again.

Finally, Peter reached in and placed a firm hand under him, lifting Toby's back end until he was standing. Peter reached both arms under and lifted him down from the rear of the vehicle. The sharp, coarse gravel dug into Toby's dry, cracked paws. He shifted his weight to find relief on the precarious stones.

The tailgate slammed closed with a thud that startled the jittery dog. Peter took a few short steps towards the concrete building and the leash extended, pulling taut against Toby's collar. At a slight tug on the leash, Toby took one step and then two. The leash tugged again, and then he took a third step and a fourth and a fifth. The gravel was unfamiliar and hurt his paws. The cacophonous barking grew louder with each step closer.

On the fifth step, the smells hit Toby's nose with the force of a summer storm: a thousand smells rushing forth all at once. His nostrils overflowed with the stench of urine and feces, bird droppings, the spray of mating cats, mold and mildew, dust and rust, decay, and a world of other scents the young dog had never experienced. All of it smelled unwelcoming and inhospitable.

It was all too much for Toby to take in. He crumbled to the gravel, the rocks digging into his underbelly. He began to quiver uncontrollably and urinate, the yellow liquid spilling unconsciously over his leg.

The man let out a disgruntled sigh, loosening the leash and coming to lift Toby from the ground. The boy pounded on the glass inside the car, still sobbing. His wails sent shivers through Toby as he lay there in a trembling heap.

Peter stepped towards the frightened dog and lifted him, the sounds of the little boy drowning away in the distance. Toby was salivating now, long strips of drool spilled from the edges of his mouth, staining Peter's checkered shirt. They reached the old gray doors set monotonously into the callous concrete walls. Deep blue paint peeled from the doors, faded into splotches of rust. As Peter pulled the door open with his free hand, the smells rushed forth at Toby even stronger now, unimpeded by the walls of the building.

The metal door whooshed past his nose, lifting the soft whiskers around his snout with the gentle wind. Just ahead, a bright orange sign read, "Owner Surrenders" with a large block arrow pointing left. Peter paused for a moment, read the sign, and pivoted left, opening a second door.

As they passed through the second door, Toby

could see that the lobby was bustling with activity, people milling around, adults and children peering blankly into the cages of cats that lined the walls. Two staff worked quickly to help a group of people ahead in line, including a young couple and an elderly woman holding a small, dirty carrier that smelled like a very sick cat.

Peter adjusted Toby in his arms as the dog had begun to sag, his limp body slipping like a shapeless form through his coiled arms. He reached over and gave Toby a couple of insincere strokes on the crown of his head that went unnoticed in the sheer terror of the moment.

Toby's senses screamed at him from all directions, overloaded with the sights, sounds, and smells of the building. It was one thing to smell the scent of a neighborhood dog on the leaves of a neighbor's shrub, but it was another entirely to be blasted in sensitive nasal membranes with age-old smells left by years of sad and desperate animals.

A young woman stepped around the counter towards Peter and spoke in a friendly tone to both he and Toby. Her pleasant tone belied a look of concern. "Hi, how can I help you?" she said to Peter, glancing at the dog in his arms.

Peter stepped forward past the old woman with the sickly cat and set Toby down on the ground. Toby's legs were like noodles and he flopped to the slick, tile ground at Peter's feet, panting and shaking.

"I need to give up *this* dog," he said, the word

"this" hanging in the air, cold and unnatural. "My wife and I are having a baby and can't give him the attention he deserves," he continued.

There was a moment of silence and the woman's face registered a brief and virtually imperceptible flash of disappointment. Her round cheeks flushed red for a moment, contrasting her sandy blonde hair that hung over a plain blue smock. "I see," she said slowly then continued after a pause. "We have several programs that may be useful if it's a financial matter including a food donation program, free neuter vouchers, and some other options," she suggested without looking at Peter. She reached across the counter to a colorful brochure which she slid across the hard wood towards Peter. "Would any assistance allow you to possibly keep your dog?" she asked, looking up at him.

"Thank you, but no. We just don't have the time for him anymore," he replied politely but unmistakably firm.

The young woman's hands were already in motion before Peter finished as she sensed what he would say. She slid a wooden clipboard towards him, placing a black pen on top as she did. "I'll need you to fill out some paperwork to give us background information on the dog, and there is a waiver on the back you will need to read and sign indicating you understand you are surrendering your animal to a public shelter and there are no guarantees of placement," she said somewhat mechanically.

Peter seemed to falter at the last words. He looked

at the papers on the clipboard for a moment. His mouth opened as if to speak, but nothing came out. Then he seemed to find the words. "You guys do adoptions here, right?" he asked, a tiny hint of indignation creeping into his tone. "So there's a pretty good chance he will find a home, isn't there?" he followed, this time with clear uncertainty.

"We're the public animal shelter of Clay County, so we're required to take any animal that comes to our door. We make every effort to adopt out animals, but occasionally, because of space limitations or behavioral issues, we unfortunately have to euthanize an animal," she replied, the words coming with a cadence borne by constant repetition.

Peter stood there silently for a long moment, staring at the paperwork. She continued. "The waiver on the back of your paperwork indicates that you understand your dog may be at risk for euthanasia."

Peter looked at the paper, flipping it front to back and back to front, digesting everything he was just told, absorbing her words. "What about the County Humane Society up on Baron Street?" he asked suddenly. "Do they put dogs down, or could I take him there?"

"The Humane Society won't take pit bulls, unfortunately. They're a private shelter; they can pick and choose what they want to take. We're run by the county, and we take everything that comes through that door," she responded, gesturing to the metal door behind him. "We do the best we can with what we've got," she added unsolicited after a short pause.

Peter put the clipboard down for a moment and looked out towards the car. He wondered what the children would think, what Sandra would say at this moment. He hadn't expected this, this process not quite what he had planned.

He looked down to his feet at Toby. The young dog was laying awkwardly on the blue-and-white colored tiles, legs splayed to one side unnaturally. He was panting rapidly, his sides rising and falling quickly with each breath. Faint streaks of urine glistened on the floor beneath his sinewy legs.

Peter looked back at the paperwork and paused a moment more.

He picked up the black pen and began to sign his name.

The voices above Toby were faint, muted in the stirring of his mind. Peter was speaking unintelligibly to the woman with the yellow hair. Toby's body was shaking so feverishly, the sounds of the cartilage of his ears reverberated in harmony with the chattering of his jaws, drowning out the conversation. He knew he had peed himself and he felt ashamed, but he could not muster the strength to rise above the foul liquid.

From the corner of his eye, he sensed the woman coming around the counter.

Her voice was soft and comforting, the gentle noise dramatically contrasting with the backdrop of yelping and pained howls in the background.

"Hiiiii, honey," she spoke, crouching down just a

few feet away from him.

Toby stared straight ahead into the back of Peter's legs, allowing himself only a sideways glance at the lady.

"Are you so scared?" she asked, the pitch of her words rising as she slowly extended her hand towards him. "It's ok, honey. I know you're scared," she continued, moving her hand ever so closer to Toby.

He wanted to touch her hand, the source of the soft voice, the only source of anything that wasn't foul and miserable in this place. But he was so scared. He turned his head away from the hand, but his eyes were still fixed sideways on her.

"He's a friendly dog, he's just scared," said Peter from above, glancing downwards at Toby, his tone flat and unemotional. He turned back and continued the paperwork.

The blonde lady looked up at Peter as he turned his back, the disdain in her eyes betraying her congenial personality. She said nothing.

She slowly pulled her hand back and sat down on the dirty floor, cross-legged and fully committed to the dog. She continued speaking to Toby in short sentences, the tone always pleasant and patient. He was a good boy, she told him, she would take care of him and get him all set up with a place to live, she said. She would get him a bowl of food and some water to drink.

She went on and on for several minutes, her voice soothing and tranquil, her hand always just inches away. After several long minutes, Toby began to trust her and the words she spoke. The shivering in his body began to calm. Slowly and cautiously, he turned his head towards her. She reached out again and touched him. Toby ducked his head under her hand, guiding her fingers to the bridge of his nose to scratch. And she did.

Peter had finished writing and stood towering anxiously above Toby, watching the scene unfold. Toby could still sense him there and that he was growing impatient, perhaps frustrated with this turn of events. *Perhaps he doesn't like the lady touching me*, Toby thought. *Perhaps he's ready for us to leave and go home.*

"How long have you had him?" the woman asked without looking up, continuing to scratch the bridge of Toby's nose.

"We got him about 6 months ago. The kids wanted a dog," he said as if deflecting the guilt of his actions to some unseen children. "He really is a good dog. We just don't have the time for him anymore. I'm sure someone else will do much better by him."

Putting her hands on the ground behind her, the woman slowly pushed herself upwards, taking care not to startle the young dog. She gave a smile down at Toby and stepped behind the counter to study the paperwork. She flipped the pages back and forth as she read silently. When she finished, she set the clipboard down on her desk and placed the pen back in the pen holder beside a dozen others.

"Do you want his collar?" she asked Peter.

"No, he can keep it," he replied.

"Alright, you're all done then," she said without emotion, fastening the end of Toby's leash to a metal hook just under the counter.

Peter stood there in silence for just a moment, looking down at Toby who still lay splayed across the floor, panting. He bent forward at the waist and leaned towards the dog, offering a sympathetic stroke to Toby's head.

"You be a good boy, Toby. I know you're going to find a home you can be happy in," his words came, perfunctory and hollow. He scratched him quickly behind one ear, stood upright, and turned to leave.

"Thank you," he said to the woman, only half-turning as he stepped for the door. The door swung open and then closed again, the swift breeze rippling the fur on Toby's back.

The woman waited a moment after the door closed, standing with both hands braced on the desk, watching the man leave. As the door slowly ground to a halt, the squeaking of the rusted hinges gave way to the labored sounds of Toby's panting. She stepped out from behind the counter and knelt next to Toby.

"I'm sorry, sweetheart," she said, her words somehow even softer and gentler than before. "I promise we'll do our best," she said, gently rubbing under his chin with the palm of her hand. She stood again, the stiff blue smock crackling with her motions.

She walked behind the counter once more, clicked a microphone, and spoke, "Derrick to the front for intake. Derrick to the front for intake." The loud noise from the ceiling startled Toby, and he pressed his back to the counter just as the woman came around again, kneeling again before him.

Without saying a word, she reached under his chin. The jingling of tags resonated in Toby's ears as he stared at her, half frozen in fear, half pleading for comfort. His collar tugged and pulled for a moment, and then the jingling stopped. As the woman pulled back her thin hands, he saw she was holding his tags.

It was at that moment that the gravity of the situation truly set in, and Toby could sense the finality of the moment.

No more would he have a home of his own.

No more would he visit the park.

No more would he ever see Frankie.

No more would the man and woman walk with him.

No more would the boy scratch behind his ears and talk to him so gently.

Even by himself at night in the backyard, he had a family.

Now, he was truly alone.

Toby was stirred from his thoughts by a rush of air from his left as another door opened and swung closed. His body quaked harder than before. Soft, almost inaudible whines came from deep within him, sounds he had never made before.

"What's up?" came a new voice, quick but casual and kind.

"Owner surrender. Needs to be checked in," replied the woman, now unseen behind the counter. "Thanks, Derrick."

Toby looked up at the man standing before him in a pair of worn, loose-fitting jeans. He was tall and sturdy with a turquoise smock. His skin was dark, the color of cocoa, with long dreadlocks tied in a ponytail behind his angular face.

"What's up, my man?" he said, crouching down before Toby. Something about the man set Toby instantly at ease. His voice contained no judgment, no pretense, and no fear. He was warm and welcoming to the little dog who lay like a shabby puddle on the shelter floor.

As he knelt before Toby, he spoke to the yellow-haired woman who tapped at the keyboard. "What's his story?" he asked, turning over his shoulder as he spoke.

There was a pause, the silence filled only with the tapping of plastic keys, and then she spoke. "Guy said he didn't have time for him. Got him as a pup. Can't deal with him. Paperwork says a kid on the way. Same old stuff." Her voice was staccato and emotionless.

Derrick shook his head, scratching gently down Toby's side. "Alright, my man," he said.

"His name is Toby," interjected the yellow-haired woman.

"Toby," he said back, testing it out. "Alright, my man. Toby," he said, trying the name on for size. "We're gonna hook you up and get you into your new digs," he said, taking the leash from the counter and giving a gentle tug. Toby didn't move but stay hunkered into the side of the counter, lowering his head. Another gentle tug and Toby hunkered even closer to the counter.

"You gonna make me carry you, buddy?" he spoke, bending down and sliding his hands under Toby's sides, gently lifting him to his feet. "Come on, Toby. Show me how you do it." Another gentle tug of the leash.

This time Toby moved his feet slowly and unsteadily, one before the other, right over left, his crooked gait a sign of his uncertainty and fear.

Derrick was patient, letting Toby work the kinks out of his legs. Toby's eyes were wild, and his mouth was open. Slowly but surely, he walked, following Derrick across the cool, slick floor.

And so the two went in their sad parade, the tall, friendly man and the shaky, black dog. As they reached another doorway, Derrick slowly pulled the handle, making sure it didn't scare Toby on the way in.

"Here," came the woman's voice behind him, standing up and reaching out to Derrick with a piece of paper. He turned and took it from her, slipping it into a large pocket on his smock.

After a minute more, they were in a back room. The noises had subsided a bit, but the room smelled like medicine and sickness. Paint was peeling at the top corners of the wall. The room was small and enclosed with concrete walls. Small cages lined the walls, and to the right was a counter and a shiny metal table.

Derrick clipped Toby's collar to a metal hook on the wall. He pulled the papers from his smock and set them down on the counter.

"Alright, my man. We're gonna get you hooked up," he said, a smile crossing his face as he leaned down to Toby, a syringe filled with banana-colored fluid in his hand. Toby was still trembling, but he calmed being away from the lobby and in the presence of the patient man. Derrick leaned in with the syringe and gently pulled Toby's mouth open with the fingers of his left hand. Toby resisted at first, then gave way partly in trust and partly because he had little spirit to fight anymore. The yellow liquid squirted forth into Toby's mouth, and he made a sudden face, squinting his eyes and shaking his head as Derrick gently held his muzzle closed. Toby swallowed the foul-tasting gunk and Derrick released his grip, reaching to scratch Toby up and down his back in praise for what he had done.

The two continued like this for several more minutes, and Toby generally didn't seem to mind. The friendly man gave him a pair of shots and checked Toby's ears and teeth, writing information on the sheet with every step. Toby didn't like being prodded or poked, and he hadn't felt a needle as long as he could remember, but he sat and let the man go about his business. He had stopped panting and his trembling muscles finally began to relax.

The door to the room opened swiftly and the yellow-haired woman popped in. Her black nametag pinned to her rumpled smock read, MELISSA.

"How's he doing?" she asked, looking at Toby as she spoke.

"He's alright," came the reply from Derrick. "Never understood why people wanna give up on a good dog," he continued, half question, half comment.

Melissa looked at Toby and squinted her eyes, a tight smile creasing her face as she looked at him. Toby looked back blankly. She pivoted on her feet, turned and left.

"Alright, Toby. You ain't gonna like this, but we gotta get you settled in your run," said Derrick, a look of empathy crossing his face. He unhooked the collar from the counter. Toby sat up, suddenly confused by the change in tone from the man.

Derrick gave a short tug on the leash and Toby was on his feet, following him slowly out of the room and down the hall. The sounds of barking grew louder. The scents of lonely dogs crept in from every crack of every wall. Toby walked ever so slowly, hugging the wall, his tail tucked deeply between his legs. His feet barely lifted off the floor as he walked, almost instinctively silencing himself so as not to be discovered in this place he didn't belong.

Through another set of slate-colored doors they walked, the gray walls surrounding them like some impenetrable fortress. They continued, creeping along down a long hall until they came to a single door with a large, metallic knob of a handle. The sign posted on the door — the one Toby couldn't read — said, IN-

# CHASING THE BLUE SKY

TAKE AND HOLDING — STAFF ONLY.

# CHAPTER 6

The rusted chain-link fence vibrated before Toby's eyes and his stomach grew sick. His constant and uncontrollable shivering caused the narrow kennel to sway back and forth before him. The walls, once painted white, were cracked and peeled, the exposed cinderblock conjuring a blend of dusty cream and drab gray in the tiny cell.

The floor reeked of urine and excrement, years of dog matter hosed clean a thousand times but still lingering on every inch of concrete. Measuring just five-feet-long by three-feet-wide, the space was claustrophobic to all but the tiniest of dogs, and Toby was no longer a tiny dog.

He quivered mercilessly, his mouth open, his body slouched inelegantly in a half-sitting heap. His mind was closed to all but the immediate stimuli, unable to do much more than stimulate his body's harsh physical reactions to his current predicament. The sweat-soaked fur of his chest rose and fell almost spastically, his wide mouth panting deeply. The short whiskers on his snout flickered upwards with each forceful exhale.

He sat in his heap half-on a rectangular slab of plastic, the edges smooth and the top grooved for traction. To his right sat a metal bucket, attached to the chain-link with a smooth metal clip, the only thing not showing signs of rust from years of use. Behind him, a narrow opening in the concrete sat just below a rusty metal plate attached to a long, frayed piece of wire that ran up into the ceiling like some long-dead and decaying serpent.

On the other side of the fence stood Derrick, his soft words lost in the void. Moments before, Toby had been walking with Derrick through the building. The initial shock of the lobby's commotion, the strange yellow medicine, and the pin-pricks slowly pushed into the corners of his mind by the kindness of this new friend. They had walked through the building to this noisy room and the fear began to grow once again. Then Derrick had hoisted him upwards, the ground falling below his feet, and Toby found himself in this tiny space. Derrick had given a short stroke over Toby's forehead that did little to soothe him before closing the chain-link between them.

The kennel was noisy, echoing with the barks of countless unseen dogs. For several long minutes, Toby sat there and shivered, surrounded in the self-preserving silence of his mind. The overpowering smells and sights had seemingly drowned out the clamorous noises around him, but gradually the noises began to trickle into his ears. He began to process the sound of dozens of dogs barking — loud, aggressive, and desperate. He could sense that they were barking at him from everywhere, through the walls and behind the doors.

"Hey! What are you doing here?!"

"Look, a new guy!"

"Hey, you! Come over here!"

"He'll never last here!"

Toby had never been so terrified in his life. His mind stumbled and stuttered, and he sat staring blankly past Derrick, mouth agape and eyes as wide as saucers. Derrick's mouth was still moving as he stood before the quaking dog.

"It's alright, buddy," he said softly, his fingers poking inside the chain-link, beckoning Toby to draw nearer. "Don't listen to these other dogs. Some of them are busted. You're gonna be ok, buddy. We'll get you up front before too long," he went on.

"Hey, new guy! Where'd you come from?!"

"Look at me, over here! Look, look, look!"

Derrick's figure before him was a dim blur, the long dreadlocks blending strangely with the gray slate of the door far behind him. Toby's stomach was queasy now, and he felt that he might retch and vomit at any time. He slumped to the cold ground of the cell, no longer a half-sitting heap, but now a furry, pulsating pile on the concrete floor. He tried to lay his head down on his paws, but the nerves kept him raising and lowering his head over and over, the drool pooling in the corners of his mouth. He looked like some marionette whose master tugged and pulled at the strings just out of sight, his wide-mouthed pant a sad substitute for a comical smile.

Derrick soothed the crown of his head with his fingers once more and turned to leave, but Toby barely noticed. Toby leaned forward and made a soft gagging noise, the remnants of grocery-shelf dog food — his breakfast at the house — spilled out before him in a brown liquid puddle speckled with half-digested chunks.

When he looked up again, Derrick had vanished, and he could see down the long hallway before him to the gray metal door, its window papered over with layers of tape. Only a faint glimmer of the lights from the hallway beyond shone through the thin paper.

The barking and howling had quieted a bit since Derrick left, but it was still boisterous. Toby's mind throbbed with the realization that he had nowhere to run to escape the sounds. He lay there cloaked in the howling.

For the better part of an hour, Toby lay motionless in his cell. It was only when the door suddenly lurched open that his body instinctively moved. He jumped to his feet and cowered back into the corner of the concrete enclosure, tucked his tail tightly behind him, and tilted his head sharply downward, attempting to avoid contact with whatever was coming through that door.

"Hi, Toby," came a familiar voice. He looked up with a faint recollection in his eyes. "How are you adjusting? Is it scary back here?" spoke the small yellow-haired woman named Melissa in her blue smock. She had a set of paper bowls in her right hand. As she came closer, Toby could smell her: the mix of human perfume and the stench of a dozen strange dogs emitting a peculiar aroma.

The metal chain that kept his enclosure secure clinked and jingled as she fiddled with the lock for a moment. Suddenly the door opened just a crack, and she leaned forward and slid the red-and-white paper bowls in front of him. She nudged them forward with her fingers so that he could smell the food, a pungent and curious stew of dry and wet food.

"You want a little bit of supper, buddy?" she said as she pushed the chain-link gate open wider.

Toby could sense the presence of the dog pacing back and forth in the kennel to his left. His shadow moved across Melissa's right shoulder, back and forth, back and forth.

As Melissa sat looking at him patiently, Toby let out a faint whine, unsure of what to do. His stomach grumbled, and he was very hungry, but he had no comfort in this food or in this place.

"You eat whenever you're ready, Toby," she said, his name rolling off her tongue with an uncommon familiarity. The sound of his name from this stranger caught him off guard, but it brought him some unexpected comfort.

Melissa gently closed the gate to the kennel and latched the security chain. She gave Toby a sympathetic look and turned to leave, walking briskly down the hall the way she had come. The large metal door closed softly as she guided it to its rest, giving one last glance towards him as she did.

Toby was left to the sounds of the kennel and a few scattered barks on either side of him. They no longer seemed directed at him but rather generally seeking attention from someone, anyone. Somewhere up above him, he could hear the distant flutter of a bird's wings. He lifted his head slightly and looked up, the ceiling of his cell covered with the same rusted fencing. High above in the rafters many feet beyond the wire fencing that imprisoned him, Toby could see a small brown bird, a common wren, perched on a worn iron beam. The little bird was looking at him, its head tilted sharply in the way birds do, studying the new arrival with a keen curiosity. After a moment, it fluttered its tiny speckled wings and flew upwards towards an opening in a large vent and out into the pale blue sky above, free from the caged animals below.

Toby sat for several long moments, still shaking and then scooted himself off the plastic bed squarely onto the concrete floor. It was cold and rough, and a chill permeating through his paws and underbelly. He sensed there was little comfort to be had in this place.

"Hey," a voice called. "Hey, new guy."

Toby's ears perked up at the sounds coming from somewhere beyond the raised metal door at the back of his kennel. He twisted his head to try and place the location.

"Come here," the voice demanded.

Toby sat for a moment, thinking, still quivering.

Eventually, curiosity got the better of him, and he turned in his kennel, half-standing, half-scooting until his head was aimed at the little opening. On the other side, he could see a shadow cast long across the concrete.

"Come out here," the shadow said once more.

Toby shook even more, not knowing what to do. He wished the lights were off and that his whole cell was cloaked in darkness. He wanted to curl up and just wish away this whole awful experience. But no matter how much he wished, he knew it would do no good. And so he stood on wobbly legs and approached the opening, slowly ducking his head beneath the metal door.

Poking his head cautiously through the opening for the first time, he saw a small, concrete slab of floor before him, completely enclosed by chain-link fencing on both sides and above, about the same size as his cell. Toby sensed this was the outdoor area where he was supposed to do his bathroom business. The fencing on the sides scared him. He much preferred the concrete walls that kept him enclosed and hidden from view where no one could see him shivering.

He heard footsteps to the right just on the other side of the chain-link, slowly pacing back and forth. He heard low, deep breaths, the kind that come from an older dog who was breathing out the last, musty remnants of a long life.

Fueled by youthful curiosity, Toby mustered up a small dose of courage and poked just the tip of his nose and eyes through the opening in the concrete. He moved hesitantly and fearfully.

A single eye met his gaze, and he jerked back suddenly, not expecting to see what he had seen. Without thinking, he poked his head forward again. The face and eye had been startling but not uninviting.

"Come talk to me."

Toby took a small, unsure step forward with his right front paw, and then he drew it back. He paused for a moment and then gingerly placed the paw forward again, taking one step and then another. He ducked his head and crouched his body until he was awkwardly standing, stooped low, half-way on the concrete slab.

His eyes were unsteady and his gaze unsure, but slowly as he dipped through the opening he lifted his head and looked on the other side of the chain-link fence that separated his kennel from the one beside him.

There before him on the other side of the chain-link stood a very large dog, his body clearly old and worn, but tall and still muscled. His coat was chocolate but dull and faded. The tips of his fur bore whitish ends, and his legs and joints were covered with patches of bare, hardened skin and thickened scabs. Toby stared at his face, unaware even that he was staring. This was the closest he had been to another dog since he last played with Frankie, and this dog was far from Frankie. The dog looked back with one eye of amber yellow surrounding a jet-black pupil, the yellow streaked with traces of black from years of age. His other eye was nothing more than a fleshed-over socket, a remnant of some grievous injury. His ears stood tall, sharp, and jagged, having been cut to points many, many years ago. They were nicked and scratched, scabbed and healed many times over. The dog was old yet imposing, but his aura struck Toby as strangely peaceful.

"Welcome, youngster," he said, his voice deep and strong.

Toby continued to stare, unable to muster any response.

"We've all been through what you're going through, every one of us in here," said the large dog. "It's easier for some more than others, some of us that..." He paused mid-sentence and then continued, "have had a harder life. I'm guessing you haven't had too tough a life, have you?" he asked.

Toby dropped his gaze, he knew his world was nothing compared to what the old dog had been through. "No, sir. I suppose it could be worse," said Toby sheepishly, looking at the concrete floor.

The old dog looked at Toby, letting him collect his thoughts.

"I don't like it here, though," Toby added.

The old dog paused for several long seconds and then responded. "None of us do, son. It's not a matter of liking it. It's a matter of getting used to it," he replied, a hint of empathy in his tone.

Toby merely nodded, having nothing to offer in return. "What is this place?" he asked after a long pause.

"This here is the public animal shelter. Where all the bad dogs go or the dogs no one wants anymore. Some of 'em get lucky and get out of here. Some of 'em don't," said the old dog.

With these last words, the old, brown dog scanned the rows of kennels on either side of them. Toby followed his expression, noting the many empty kennels along their top row.

"H-h-how long have you been here?" Toby sputtered, suddenly growing more nervous.

"Too long. Too long," came the reply, as the old dog shook his head from side to side in a long, slow arch. Then he looked upwards into the open sky towards the bank of gray clouds settling over the kennel. "Coming up on six months now. Longest of any dog on this block," he continued.

Toby felt a rush of anxiety rise within him, the length of time clearly catching him off guard. "How did you get in here?" he asked.

The old dog scratched the side of his face down the chain-link fencing and rubbed his back on the edge of the concrete by the entrance to his cell. "They say I'm a bad dog. A biter. Dangerous. You know?"

Toby looked away nervously.

The old dog continued. "I never bit anybody that didn't need to be bit, nobody that never beat me, or kicked me, or chained me up. Them's the people that need to be bit. Wound me up in here just waitin' on my turn," he added, looking again towards the clouds as he spoke.

Toby remained silent, deferring to the older dog.

"The name's Oscar," he said once again brushing his face against the chain-link dividing them. "And you are?"

"Toby," replied the smaller dog after a moment of hesitation.

Oscar continued to stare at him thoughtfully. The depth of the yellow in his lone eye was like a wise and watchful beacon.

"How did you end up in here, kid?" said Oscar

"I-I-I... I don't really know what happened," stammered Toby.

Oscar nodded several times, deep in thought and then spoke, "That's how it often goes, it seems."

"I had things good for a while. I had some kids that loved me... and a family, too." Toby thought for a moment and then added, "And a friend named Frankie. But they're all gone now..."

Toby's gaze was distracted by some commotion at the far end of the kennel. A pair of dogs barked as the small brown wren flittered across the ceiling, looking for scraps. Oscar saw Toby's attention shift to the little bird.

"That one," said Oscar, looking towards the little wren. "Been around as long as I've been here. Comes and goes as he pleases. Don't know why any bird would want to be in this place." He paused for a moment, pensive and then continued, "Maybe he just likes to see how the rest of us live."

Toby watched the wren curiously as it flittered around nimbly through the rafters. Occasionally, the little bird would land on the concrete floor to peck at some unseen dropping or crumb and then rise suddenly back towards the safety of the ceiling.

"He may be in here, but he ain't one of us. No man's keeping that one in a cage," Oscar said, the admiration unmistakable in his voice. He paused for a moment and added longingly, "He's free."

*He is truly free*, thought Toby. *No place like this could ever contain that little bird.* What Toby wouldn't give to fly away with that little bird, somewhere beyond these walls and away from the dampening sadness of the place.

"I want to go back home. Back to Mason and Samantha. Back to my bed…" he said, almost pleading to no one in particular.

"I'm sorry, kid," Oscar replied, his words laced with an unspoken acknowledgment that the young dog would never return home. "You're here now. And there's some things you need to learn if you want to get out of this place."

Toby sat back and rested on his haunches, slowing growing comfortable in the presence of the old dog. "I do," he said, the hopefulness betrayed by the sadness in his voice.

And so the two dogs spoke well into the night, Oscar sharing the wisdom of a dog who had much to give. Eventually, Toby nodded off, exhausted from the long, eventful day. He lay on his side halfway out of his kennel, snoring softly. The lights of the shelter flickered off inside and the shelter went dark. Across the chain-link, Oscar lay down on the concrete facing Toby and closed his eye to sleep.

# CHAPTER 7

T he irregular flickering of lights coming to life and the sounds of heavy switches being flipped roused Toby from his deep slumber. He woke to find himself curled tightly in a ball on the hard, plastic platform, his nose pressed against the dry, chipped concrete. He must have moved during the night, though the sleep deprived him of the memory. For a brief second, he didn't remember where he was, but it took only a moment for the last vestiges of sleep to depart and the reality of his present predicament to seep back into his consciousness. He stood on stiff, cramped legs and arched his back upwards. While the conversation with Oscar and the night of sleep had seemingly cured his shivering, a deep sense of dread still clung to his bones.

Toby thought back to his words with Oscar and was thankful to have the presence of another dog at the moment, even if they were separated by the worn, rusty fence. While Oscar's background was far removed from his own, their common dilemma forged a shared bond. Oscar's story and scars were a testament to his survival, and Toby sensed he would have to learn much from the old dog if he hoped to escape this place.

The halogen lights above flickered and buzzed with an electronic crackle, slow to fully come to life in the concrete catacomb of the animal shelter. Eventually, one by one, they all came on, shining harshly onto the stone and metal, turning the obscuring darkness into awakened dreariness. On the concrete floor below, small puddles of water pooled here and there, reflecting the bright lights back from whence they came. The tiny, tan-and-brown wren flickered down from the rafters, searching for a stray bit of kibble. The quickness of his wings was in stark contrast to the vapid scene below.

Across the long kennel, there wasn't a single bark or whimper. All remained silent. Toby could sense many dogs around him though despite the quiet. It was clear to him that they had settled into a morning routine after many nights in this place. To him, this was his first morning alone, fully surrendered to the great concrete walls.

With the creak of worn hinges, the door ahead opened and in stepped a woman. He had not seen this woman before. She was younger than Melissa, the yellow-haired woman from yesterday. This woman's hair was long and dark and tied tightly into a ponytail. She was small and slight with fair skin. Against her porcelain skin, Toby noticed a series of old, brownish bruises on her arms. She looked up towards the kennels as she entered, her eyes glancing past Toby. He noticed that her gaze was firm but kind, and this set Toby somewhat at ease. She slowly guided the door closed, doing her best to keep from waking the dogs, even making a frown when the latch made a soft click. As she stepped across the floor, Toby noticed that she was wearing a pair of funny-looking boots, tall and olive-green, almost over her knees. She strode softly, almost creeping into the kennel, her face forming into a smile as she approached the wakening dogs. As she drew closer, she directed herself to Toby's left, towards Oscar's kennel. Her strides were long but quiet.

Toby could hear the soft snoring from Oscar's kennel, but before the woman could reach him, a bark sounded down the run, a loud, anxious, and announcing bark.

"Shhhhhh! Julius!" said the woman, half whispering, half shouting, her voice bearing the hints of a funny twang. She placed her finger to her mouth and looked down the kennel to somewhere that Toby could not see.

Toby could hear the rustling in the kennel next to him, the sounds of aching old bones gathering and rising as Oscar pulled his head from curled limbs. He woke and stood to face his visitor.

"Hi, Oscar," she said. Toby stood and angled himself so that he could watch her. On her clean dark t-shirt was a nametag that said, ANNE. As she spoke, she reached her small hand towards the chain-link and poked two thin fingers through to scratch Oscar on the top of his head as he bowed to accept the gesture. She rested her face against the fencing, her affection for the older dog obvious in her expression and her tone. "Good morning, my little man," she went on, speaking to him in a soft, warm voice.

Oscar stood now, at his full height, towering above the small woman. He let out a morning groan and stretched the achiness from his tired muscles and joints. He gave one big shake, the skin on his sides rippling up and down before settling. The metal ring on his tagless collar clinked once against the buckle.

From Oscar's cell, Toby could hear welcoming noises as the older dog grunted softly and pawed towards the woman across from him. As she continued petting him through the chain-link, she looked slowly to her left, making eye contact with Toby who stood at attention in his kennel, unsure of her intentions. His wide eyes stared back at her, unblinking.

"Well, hello, there," she said, her voice chipper and heartfelt. "What's your name?"

Anne stepped away from Oscar, continuing to scratch him until her hand pulled away from his snout. She approached Toby's kennel and lifted the soggy paper card attached to the front of his cage with a metal clip and began to read quietly to herself. Toby could hear Oscar pacing in the run next door.

"Toby, huh?" she said, her tone deep with inquisitiveness. "Well where did you come from, sweetheart?" she asked as she leaned her face to the kennel.

Toby began to tremble at the sudden attention,

pacing backward in his kennel and tucking into the corner against the concrete. He began to shiver again, a slow, building shiver. Even on the coldest winter's nights, he had never shivered like this. The foreboding fear of this place frightened him to his core.

Anne unlatched the chain on the kennel and slowly flipped up the latch, carefully reaching a long, slender hand into his run. She stopped her hand a foot from Toby's nose so that he could smell her. He inhaled the scents of her hand, a mixture of cleaning chemicals and dog food. She stood motionless, her hand hovering a comfortable distance from him. He leaned, closing the distance and allowing the smells to permeate his nostrils, a mundane bit of stimuli in an otherwise monotonous environment.

After he had sniffed for a moment, she slowly lifted her hand and reached to one side of his face, Toby's eyes following her the whole time as he hunkered down, ducking his head. Her hand made contact with his fur and began to caress him behind one ear. Toby could feel the fear gradually subsiding with each stroke of her hand. She began scratching at the base of his ear, deep into the soft cartilage, and after a moment, his eyes began to close, and his head dipped down to the plastic platform.

"Shhhhhhh," she whispered softly, a small breeze from her lips brushing the fur on Toby's crown. Toby continued to relax, giving himself to the unexpected comfort. "It's ok, Toby. I'm your friend now," she said, the truth unquestionable in her words.

Anne continued massaging Toby for several more minutes, almost putting him into a deep and tranquil trance. When she finished, she gently caressed the crown of his head with her palm and then slowly pulled away with a familiar "Shhhhhhh." Toby opened his eyes slowly when her hand was removed, and he lay there calmly looking at the woman. She returned his look with a warm smile and lightly closed the gate to his kennel.

"I'll come back to see you later, friend," she said. Toby hoped she meant it. "You too, Oscar," she said, casting a short look to her right. She stepped back, turned, and headed towards the door in her tall green boots. There was a single, sharp bark down the kennel to her right. "And of course, you, Julius," she responded to some unseen dog.

For the rest of the day, Toby and Oscar sat side by side — separated by chain-link — in the outer areas of their kennels. Throughout the day, Toby learned a great deal from Oscar. The old dog had a depth of character and wisdom that Toby had never encountered in his young life. His wisdom, though, was tainted with a profound sadness that seemed only to lift momentarily when he shared stories with the younger dog.

Toby ate two meals that first day, both times a hard, dried kibble that only half-filled his bowl. His nervousness quelled his hunger though, and he only finished a portion of each bowl, leaving the rest to sit. Although Oscar was a much larger dog, he received the same size portions, and Toby wished he could share the rest of his meal. Oscar encouraged Toby to finish his bowl as they would not get another meal for many more hours, but Toby never did.

There were only a handful of other dogs in the kennel space. Toby learned from Oscar that this was the "Holding Area" that held dogs who were either brand new to the animal shelter or who could not be moved to the "Adoption" area just yet.

Toby wondered how Oscar had been here for six months. Why had he not been moved to the other area?

Oscar only answered that he had long since accepted his fate and knew that he would spend the rest of his days in this kennel. Over those long six months, he had seen many dogs come and go. Toby would soon go too, he said. He told Toby that he was "adoptable" and would be moved to a different kennel before too long. He reassured Toby that most of the other dogs that came through moved on quickly. Oscar knew there were no long-term friendships to be had here. Everyone came and went.

Except for Julius, that was.

Oscar told Toby that Julius had come from the same home as he did. But the two didn't get along these days and were separated now by several kennels. From the outdoor area of his cell, Toby could see Julius through the fencing, far away in the distance, his body obscured by the rusted diamonds of the chain-link. He was almost equally brown and white, the two colors alternating splotches of fur across his muscular frame. Julius was much smaller than Oscar and several years younger. Toby could sense a great deal of anxious energy in him brewing beneath the surface with no means to escape. He seemed to bark at anything that moved and constantly paced back and forth behind his chain-link, growling low at anyone who passed.

"He wasn't always like this," Oscar had told Toby. While the two dogs never got along in their former home, Julius had been different then. The two had lived side-by-side, he had explained, in the tall grass of a shaded backyard, each chained to their own thick tree, unable to touch the other but always visible. Julius had been calmer then, he seemed to have accustomed to the routine of life on a chain. Then one day for reasons Oscar could not explain, people in blue uniforms with wide black belts and electronic devices that crackled and spoke came and took them away. They took their owner too, his hands behind his back in rings of shiny metal. And they were brought here where they had been ever since. After only a short time here, Julius began to change. He grew frustrated and anxious. He would flip his metal food bowls, clanking them around his concrete cell with his paws. He would splash the water out of his deep bucket with his nose, pouring it down the front of his kennel onto the ground below. He would pace menacingly inside his cell and gnaw his flattened teeth on the rusted fencing. Oscar tried to sooth his old yard-mate, but the younger dog became increasingly aggressive and would fight him at the fence until they moved him several kennels away. Now Julius sat alone, the spaces on either side of him as empty as his spirit.

Oscar's tale saddened Toby. He couldn't see well through the tangle of fencing separating the two, but occasionally Julius would make eye contact and stare hard, his brown eyes filled with a deep anger and frustration. He would sometimes bark and circle the concrete for hours before finally slumping to the ground in a heap until morning came and he would begin again.

"He's gone mad in this place," said Oscar, the depth of his sorrow palpable in the words.

# CHAPTER 8

T he week that followed dragged on endlessly. Toby was slowly learning to adjust to this new situation and having Oscar nearby helped him, but his fear never completely subsided. Each time the door would open, he cowered in the back corner of his kennel. Sometimes it was a kennel worker coming to deliver food or fill the old water pails. Other times it was a new dog being brought in, almost always scared and shivering. And sometimes it was a worker escorting someone else up and down the rows, the new person always looking deeply into the kennels as if searching for something or someone. Whatever they were looking for back there, they never found it.

Toby spent most of his days hunkered down in his kennel, avoiding the cool winds, usually only laying outside when the sun rose where it's amber beams dispersed by the chain-link above into geometric patterns across the concrete. Oscar would usually lay outside with him and the two would share the few hours of sunshine together, one old and one young under a common sun. While Oscar was outwardly confident,

Toby could tell that deep inside, his spirit was beginning to break down.

Over the last few days, a handful of dogs had been brought into the holding area to join them. Once there was a terrified Spaniel trembling under his regal fur. Toby saw him just once as he entered and then again a day later when a worker came to get him, saying, "You're going back home now." Toby felt out of place here, but the Spaniel was even farther from any world he had ever known. *But did any dog really "belong" here?* Toby wondered to himself.

The woman with the name tag that said ANNE had been exceptionally kind to Toby. Each day she came and comforted him and Oscar simultaneously, speaking soft words to the both of them, one set of fingers through each of their fences, her head shifting back and forth between the kennels. She brought them hard biscuit treats and once even gave Toby a rubber toy filled with peanut butter, telling him he was a "good boy" for taking it slowly from her hand.

And Julius was still ever present down the row barking at anything and everything that moved or made a sound. He was clearly getting worse, his frustration and anxiety evident from several kennels away. Anne would usually visit with Julius after she had comforted Toby and Oscar, but it never seemed to quell his restlessness.

"Not much longer, buddy. Soon you'll be free and away from this place, somewhere happy. You can run and bark as much as you like," she said one time, although Toby didn't know what any of it meant.

Toby always noticed that when Anne would pass on her way out the door after visiting with Julius, her eyes were often moist and wet. She wiped at them with the edge of her collar and avoided eye contact with him or Oscar as she left the holding area. Oscar would usually make a soft, low whimper, almost a deep humming noise, as Anne would pass. She would simply pass them looking down at the floor, turn sharply at the corner, walk through the door, and close it softly behind her.

The man named Derrick paid the dogs visits as well. Melissa did too. Toby was fond of these workers; they had comforted him and been patient with him through his time here. He sensed that they were fond of him too. Everyone was fond of Oscar, even the other kennel workers who Toby didn't know. Not one would pass his kennel without a smile and a kind word.

Towards the end of the week, the door to the holding area began to open just like it did a hundred times a day. Toby could hear the scuttling of claws and feet on the other side: a newcomer trying to get traction on the slick floor.

As the door pushed all the way open, Toby could see Derrick, his left arm holding the door open while his right gently tugged on one end of a blue nylon leash.

At the end of the leash was a trembling and frightened dog — one of the most beautiful dogs Toby had seen. She was tall and lean. Her coat was long and lush;

her fur was a flaxen gold. Her eyes were a deep caramel color. From this distance, she looked to be only
slightly younger than Toby.

As she stood in the opening of the doorway, she
swayed from side to side, her long legs trembling beneath her silky coat. Derrick waited for her patiently
with one hand on the door and the other on the leash.
Oscar and Toby were both standing at the front of their
cells. They watched as she sank to her haunches, resting across the aluminum track of the doorway. Down
the far end of the kennel, Julius began his deep barking. Toby could hear him pacing and clawing at the
wire fencing.

Toby wished he could quiet Julius; he was only
making this new dog more nervous. He remembered
the barking when he entered and the panic that stirred
in him. He could hear other feet shuffling around in
their kennels at the arrival of the new visitor. Below
him and to his right, Nemo, a mangy hound dog who
had arrived a few days ago, let out a pair of short
howls. Farther to the right, Terrible Thomas, a wiry
black mutt of unknown origin, scratched feverishly at
his kennel. Oscar had said that Thomas was a "biter"
too.

The new dog was shaking in fear, still prone in the
doorway. Toby knew exactly what she was going
through. He let out a short yip of encouragement, the
friendliest bark he could muster to let her know it
would be alright. Her eyes stared wildly at the hard
concrete, and she sat motionless aside from the shak-

ing. She had shut down.

The sight brought Toby back to his arrival many days before. *You can do it*, he said to her in his mind. *You'll be in a kennel soon and have some walls to protect you. Just a little bit farther. You can do it.*

Oscar pressed his nose against the grating, carefully watching the new arrival struggle across the doorway. He'd watched this scene unfold many times before. Some dogs, like Nemo, were so slow and oblivious that they sauntered in unburdened by the thousand sounds and smells and took their place in the kennel like it was nothing. But for most, this was the process, the frightening, terrifying manifestation of their arrival in a most unwelcome place.

After a minute, Derrick bent over and scooped the golden dog up in his arms, his long dreadlocks falling off his broad shoulders and brushing against her silken fur. He started to walk forward with her cradled gently in his arms. The intensity of Julius' barking increased; he now laid eyes on the new dog. From his cell, there came a horrible, deep growl followed by three hard, rapid barks that pierced deep into Toby's ears. Toby watched the eyes of the new dog sink backward in her head, the wave of fear and panic engulfing her.

For the first time since his arrival, he let out a single sharp, corrective bark directed towards Julius. "Quiet down!" he yelled. The attempt was lost on Julius who was focused only on the new dog and continued a series of sharp barks, punctuated by low growls, the blacks of his pupils turned sideways, his eyes wide and white.

"Julius! Knock it off!" shouted Derrick suddenly, turning over his shoulder towards the barking dog as he took a few steps forward. Julius barked once more and stopped, though the low growl continued.

Toby heard the gate open next to him as Derrick came close, sliding the fear-stricken dog into the kennel on her side. Toby pressed his nose against the front of his kennel and shifted his gaze as far sideways as he could. He could just make out a small edge of her golden fur pressed completely flat on the ground of her kennel. He let out a short whimper.

"There you go, girl. I'll get you some food and water and maybe even a blanket," said Derrick, his words coming slow and labored as he caught his breath. He latched the gate and turned towards the supply room just down the hall.

As Derrick left through the door, the kennel grew silent. Even Julius had ceased his incessant barking. The new dog's kennel to Toby's right was silent. He understood what she was going through; the common fear still lingered fresh in his mind. He went outside into the open area to see if he could see through her small doorway into the kennel. Through the opening in the concrete, he could just see some wisps of her long yellow tail, shaking as her unseen body trembled beyond the concrete.

He let out three short yips to let her know that he was here, just like Oscar had done for him. She didn't respond. Toby whimpered. He wished he could help somehow. He wanted to break through the chain-link divider and comfort her. He wanted to tell her that she would make it, just like he had.

Behind him, he could hear Oscar pacing, and he turned to look. The old dog looked largely unaffected by the events that had unfolded — he'd been through this too many times before.

But Oscar looked Toby in the eye and his expression was clear: *Help her as I helped you*

For the next several hours, Toby lay outside his kennel in the open space beneath the clouded sun, his face resting against the fencing separating his kennel from that of the new dog. He did not whimper, he did not whine. He sat, waiting patiently and calmly, an unthreatening invitation for her to come and visit.

He could see very little through the small opening in the concrete. At first, he could see only a tail, and as he moved farther back in his run, a bit of her hindquarters. She appeared to be pressed against the inside of her kennel, clinging tightly to the concrete wall just as he had done. There were periodic spasms of fear in her legs marked by the rippling of her golden fur.

The day came and went like that. Derrick, Melissa, and even Anne all came periodically to check on the dogs, particularly this new one. Toby heard them call her "Marilynn," and she clearly knew her name. Every time they would call it, she responded with some subtle motion. Toby guessed she had been some family's dog just like he had. He thought she must have lived inside too. Her coat was clean, her nails were trimmed, and she didn't have the stink of most of the dogs in the holding area.

At the end of the day, Derrick came around for his final visits. He had to coax Toby in from the outdoor area, his vigil for Marilynn now in its fourth straight hour. Oscar brushed against the kennel on the far side, signaling for Toby to go back in his run. "Maybe tomorrow," Oscar said.

Toby hesitated for a moment and then grunted as he lifted himself off the hard concrete and shuffled back into the kennel. The sounds of Julius clanking his water bucket reverberated off the concrete walls. And with that, Derrick pulled on the serpentine wire that curled into the ceiling, and the rusty metal plate covering the outdoor opening fell closed.

Toby slept little that night. Instead, he listened to the sounds of Marilynn scratching at her plastic bed and trying her best to get comfortable. Occasionally, he would whimper a reassuring noise to let her know he understood her plight.

Morning came and with it came the unfortunate sight of Roland, another one of the kennel workers. Roland was far from friendly towards the dogs. The sharp spray of cold water from Roland's hose pushed Toby out into the open area as the slop of food and debris from his kennel came rushing out after him. He danced and pranced to avoid his feet getting wet with the mess. Wet feet rarely dried in this place and could make for a long, cold day. Roland was apathetic with the hose, blasting indiscriminately across the kennel.

Toby gave in and stood still, his feet and legs getting soaked with cold water that sprayed through the opening. Roland moved to the next kennel, and Toby could hear the spray on the Retriever now, he could hear her scrambling, unsure of what to do or where to go. He charged through the opening towards the front of his cell and barked at Roland, but the old, scraggly man in the dirty dungarees only turned a glare at him and shouted for him to be quiet. Toby did not listen and barked with all the ferocity he could muster. Roland turned the hose on him, a hard spray of water hitting Toby square in the chest. His legs and chest were soaked deep to his skin.

Marilynn eventually figured out her escape route and scrambled out the back of the kennel into the open area. She stood, back turned to the water. Toby sensed that she had moved, and he exited his cell for the outdoor run.

There she sat, surely a once-regal dog, now soaked and broken by her short time at the shelter. Her head was down, and her eyes were closed. The spray of cold water had flattened her long coat and her pale skin showed beneath in various patches across her body. Toby moved closer, just the thin fence separating them now. He looked at her, but she remained unmoved, her head bowed. He brushed his head against the chain-link to get her attention, but nothing stirred in her.

Toby stared at her and crooked his head. *Why won't she acknowledge me?* he wondered to himself.

He lifted one paw, then both paws and scratched

at the fence as fast as he could. The chain-link reverberated, shaking back and forth.

After a moment of scratching, she slowly turned her head towards him. Her eyes spoke more than words could say — she was wet, dejected, and afraid.

Toby looked back into her caramel eyes. He let out a yip and arched his back into his best play bow, his butt raised high in the air and his tail wagging from side to side. He held the position for a moment as Marilynn stared at him, her eyes blank and hollow. Toby slowly lowered his hindquarters and rested flat on the ground, placing his head on his paws and letting out a sigh. He sat and stared across the chain-link at nothing in particular.

"I'm here if you need me," he said, and that was all.

Marilynn stood for a moment then turned her gaze back to the concrete floor, and then slowly but surely, she lay down in her kennel, resting her side against the chain-link separating her and Toby. An energy stirred in Toby like he had not felt before, but he did his best not to startle her. Slowly, one paw at a time, he crawled the few long inches to the chain-link divider until he was beside her. Her smells came to him now. The odor of cold, stagnant water could not disguise the sweetness of her fur. Toby inhaled deeply, discerning every scent that rose from her. He could tell much from her scent and guessed her to be about a year old. He sensed that she had been well cared for, no hint of sickness in her aroma.

They sat like that all day, not speaking. Occasionally, Oscar looked on silently from the next kennel. As the day passed, Marilynn slowly warmed to the black dog, sensing a security in him and a spirit much more alive than the kennel itself. Their bond grew in the absence of words. She would occasionally look at him, making brief eye contact across the chain-link. Then she stood and took in his scents, pacing the kennel from his front to his rear. And then after a long while, she spoke to him and told Toby her story that seemed not so distant from his own.

She had been a beloved family dog. There were many small children and a nice green backyard. Somehow and for some reason unknown to her, the family had split up. The woman and children went one way and the man the other. Marilynn was caught in between. She could sense the turmoil building between the man and woman for the year leading up to the split. Things in the house were not the same. Everyone seemed agitated, and the attention they normally gave her began to fade. In the end, the woman and children moved from the house, a big truck coming one day to take their stuff away. She was alone with the man, and before long he had loaded her in the car for what she thought must be their new home. There was no new home, only this shelter.

Toby asked her about her life before the family. Where had she come from? She had come from her own family once, she said. For a brief while, she was part of a large litter of dogs in a stable somewhere on a farm that seemed so far away. She could remember people coming and taking the puppies, one by one until they were just a few remaining. When Marilynn was taken, there were just two puppies left with her mother. Her father, she barely knew, but she saw him occasionally on the farm usually in the company of other female dogs. She had no other memories of the time before the people took her. When she left with them, she thought she would be with them forever.

Toby listened intently to Marilynn's story with a combination of longing and empathy in his eyes. Her story was so familiar to his own. He wondered how many other dogs came from places like they had and wished that he could reach through the fence and press his warm body against her to comfort her. He wanted to lie beside her in the sunlight, unseparated by the metal barrier between them.

For the next several days, Toby and Marilynn spent most of their time lying side by side, pressed against each other through the chain-link, sharing warm moments, often in silence for hours. The two formed an immediate connection; their common backgrounds and their longing to be free molded their spirits together in this dark place. As the days turned to weeks, they became inseparable, the walls and fences between them doing nothing to stifle the bond they had forged.

Each morning as Roland would come with the hose, Toby would meet him at the front of the kennel, issuing warning barks and cautioning him to be gentle with Marilynn. She learned how to hide against the back corner of the concrete in the open run to avoid the brunt of the hose. This did not dissuade Toby from letting Roland know that he meant business. His barks usually earned him a quick squirt of the hose, but Toby never backed down, he would only turn his head from the hose and continue to bark at the grizzled old man.

Each day, Anne would bring them treats, usually a bucket to be distributed to the whole holding area. Toby and Marilynn would carry their treats to the fence and sit side by side, enjoying them together.

Despite his growing bond with Marilynn, Toby still worried about Oscar. The old, brown dog was quiet and stoic and showed no outward signs of sadness over the loss of attention, but Toby thought that he must be lonelier now. Despite being just feet away from Oscar, Toby could hardly help turning his attention to Marilynn. Oscar generally kept to himself these days, only occasionally walking towards the edge of Toby's kennel to check in on him. His mind seemed more focused on Julius instead anyways. The clanging of the water bucket, the scratching at the chain-link, and the pained barking all grew worse by the day. Anne had also grown more and more distant as each day passed, and while she continued to come and visit with Oscar, there was a growing sadness in her expressions, and Toby knew that Oscar sensed it too.

As the week drew on, Anne came to Toby's kennel one day with a leash. Toby grew excited at the sight; no one had come to him with a leash since the day he arrived. After some kind words to Oscar, Anne spoke to Toby in a soft voice as she always did. "Do you want to go play today, buddy?" she asked, her pitch rising at the end. "Are you going to be a good boy for me so we can move you up front?"

Toby didn't understand the words she spoke, but the presence of the leash told him this must be good news.

Behind Anne, the door opened, and Derrick came in with a leash of his own in his hand. He headed straight to Marilynn's kennel, reaching his fingers through the fence to scratch Toby quickly on the snout as he passed.

"You guys ready for your play date?" asked Derrick as he unlatched Marilynn's kennel.

Without understanding a word of what was said, Toby knew what was happening, and his whole body vibrated from side to side, his tail making broad sweeping motions across the concrete walls. Derrick lifted Marilynn to the ground, the excitement obvious in her as well. She shook twice, and some loose fur drifted to the ground. Then she did a short bounce of excitement.

Soon, Toby and Marilynn were outside in a large play yard under the watchful eyes of Derrick and Anne. Their playtime was probably only a matter of minutes, but for Toby, it felt like hours. The cool breeze and the full sun on his coat felt like magic. As soon as Anne let down the leash, he zipped across the yard from one end of the concrete to the other, his sprinting only diverted by the presence of yet another chain-link fence that bordered the play yard. Toby could tell that they were off to one side of the main building, the play yard apparently built over a small parking lot that backed up to one corner of the shelter. The walls were painted a bright yellow with a floral scene of clouds and happy dogs dancing in the grass.

Marilynn zipped past Toby as he paused to examine the yard, brushing against his coat and letting him know she was there. Derrick and Anne moved towards a picnic bench and took a seat to watch the two dogs.

It took no time at all for the two to begin a series of playful antics. At first, Toby chased Marilynn until she stopped and tumbled onto her back, rolling over and over. Toby playfully mouthed at her legs, saliva running unceremoniously down his chin. Over and over again they ran and played, each dog panting heavily but unwilling to stop.

For the time, Marilynn was herself again. The shivering dog in the kennel was momentarily left behind in the splendor of open play and her new friend. Toby was instantly invigorated as he was reminded of times with Frankie on a play date. He hoped this day would never end.

"You two look like a pretty good pair," said Anne, her dark ponytail wagging behind her head as she approached with the leash. Toby dipped and ran towards her, stopping several feet short, hoping to get her to play. She stood like a pillar and smiled at him, shaking her head from side to side.

After a moment, he realized she was not coming, dipped his head and trotted begrudgingly towards her.

"You're such a good boy, Toby. We need to find you a home," she said gently to him as she slipped the leash over his head. A short distance away, Derrick did the same for Marilynn.

And so ended their very first play date. The two dogs were led back to the holding kennel side by side like a happy couple, tails up and panting. Even back in their runs, they were relaxed, sipping water and then lounging across the chain-link in the outdoor space.

Oscar poked his head out from his kennel for a moment, gave a glance towards Toby, and then disappeared back into his run. Toby was absorbed in his own bliss to take much notice. His breathing fell into harmony with Marilynn's and the two dozed lazily on the concrete, the thin rusty wires all that separated them.

For two more days, the pair was taken out to the play yard and given time to run and play. Each day was better than the last, and the bond between them only grew stronger and stronger.

On the third day, Derrick entered the kennel with a leash and headed towards Toby's run.

"Toby, my man. It's time for you to go up front and find a home of your own," he said, the bright whites of his friendly smile contrasting against his cocoa skin.

Toby stepped forward, excited, waiting for Anne to enter the room with a leash for Marilynn, but she never did. As Derrick opened the kennel to slip the leash around him, he backed into the corner, whimpering and looking sideways towards where Marilynn was. Derrick understood immediately.

"It's alright, buddy. She's just a few days behind you. I'll be sure to make some space next to you when she comes," he said as he slipped the leash over Toby's neck and lifted him down gently to the concrete.

Toby took a second to get his footing and then looked up to Marilynn, jumping up on his back legs and pressing his nose against her cage. She pressed her nose forward as well, and Toby whimpered. The two dogs touched noses through the rusted fence before Derrick tugged the leash and led Toby towards the door.

Oscar stood stoically at the front of his kennel watching in silence, a regal statue disguised in tattered fur. In the background, Julius barked loudly, once again banging his water bowl and clawing at his kennel, a deep hopeless growling intermingled with the cacophony.

As Derrick opened the door to leave the holding area, Toby remembered Oscar. He braced his front legs to stop, sliding on the slick floor. He turned and craned his head, but Derrick's momentum pulled him forward. Oscar looked back at him with one tired but indomitable eye, never blinking as the door swung shut on its old hinges.

# CHAPTER 9

T oby adjusted quickly to his new environment. The days with Oscar and his imparted wisdom had been crucial to the young dog's survival, and he used those same lessons now in this new place.

Derrick had taken him out of the holding area and down a short hallway, through another set of doors and into a much larger kennel space. The laminated sign over the door read, "Adoptions" in dark, black letters set against a white background.

Though only a short hallway away from the old area, this new place was much bigger. As Derrick had led him into the new space, Toby noticed a stark difference in the sounds. The kennel was every bit as noisy as the prior space but somehow different. There was no clanging of metal bowls, no desperate barking. Things were somehow calmer here, the dogs slightly less forlorn and frantic. There were some woeful howls from a pair of hounds and lots of barking, but the atmosphere was not quite as hopeless as before.

Aside from the sounds, there was a noticeable difference in the physical appearance of this place. The paint on the walls seemed newer; a solid crisp white coated the walls compared to the faded cream mottled with specks of blue seeping through thousands of chips and cracks in the old place. The fencing here was newer as well. The metal occasionally reflected the bright halogen lights with a sparkle. Almost every dog that Toby passed had some sort of soft blanket or towel in their kennel, and many had tennis balls or hard rubber toys as well.

Derrick carefully guided Toby to a bottom kennel, far on the left by the entrance of the area. At first glance, it seemed more spacious than his previous cell. Toby immediately ducked his head and ran out the small opening in the concrete to check on the world outside: another small, chain-linked enclosure. The fleeting thought that freedom would greet him outside that small opening in the concrete dissipated in the millisecond it took him to pass through.

Standing outside his cell, enclosed by fencing, Toby was saddened to see that the sun couldn't quite make it through to warm the concrete floor of his enclosure as it had before. Being a bottom kennel, he found himself with a roof of concrete, and clearly another dog was above him. Looking around, he observed that from this vantage point, he could see look out the back of his fencing only a short distance away and see the outdoor play yard that he and Marilynn enjoyed so much. The sight of the yard brought a rush of memories and lifted his spirits temporarily. He hoped that someday soon he would be back there with

Marilynn, romping and galloping together on the soft grass.

As the first day passed in his new home, Toby quickly became acquainted with his neighbors on either side. First, there was Jack, a striking behemoth of a dog standing almost twice as tall at the back as Toby. His coat was a short, soft taupe with a broad pattern of white across his chest. His ears were big and floppy, hanging down the sides of his long, blackened snout. Jack appeared to be several years older than Toby, but not quite an elderly dog. His temper was mild, and he exuded a calm serenity and seemed to prefer a somber silence in his kennel over interactions with the other dogs. Very little seemed to bother Jack. He was accepting of his situation, and the greatest stress of his day was adjusting his massive frame in the cramped kennel to find a more comfortable position.

On the other side of Toby's kennel was Sadie. Her long fur, almost equally divided between black and white, was dirty and somewhat matted from many days in the shelter, but she still presented as a very regal dog. Her light blue eyes, set on patches of black fur framing a white streak up her snout, shone at Toby through the fencing. Even the drab kennel couldn't dim the twinkle in her eyes. Toby could feel her energy from across the chain-link. She longed to run and chase and herd. Sadie's interactions with Toby were always quick and nimble, always with purpose and haste. Her personality in general was upbeat, and she seemed pleased to have a young dog move in next to her. She paced her outdoor enclosure constantly, always eyeing the play yard anxiously.

The first few days in this new space passed some-what uneventfully. Toby found that there were more visitors here, not kennel workers, but new, strange people every day walking the row before the kennels and staring in, looking for something in particular. Usually Derrick, Anne, or Melissa were leading this parade of people, often pointing at various dogs in the kennels and offering various words to the new people.

Whenever Derrick would bring a new person past Toby's kennel, he would point and speak. He would say, "If you're looking for a best buddy, this is your guy." He would bend his tall frame at the waist and point at Toby, his eyes always making contact.

"What type of dog is he?" they would sometimes ask.

"He's a pit bull mix," said Derrick.

And usually their heads would lift, their eyes would avert, and they would quickly move on to the next kennel. They always seemed to linger longer in front of Jack or Sadie. Invariably whenever this hap-pened, Derrick would always linger for a moment be-fore Toby's kennel, lean over, and press his hand against the fencing for Toby to sniff, letting him know that at least he was still there.

On one occasion that first day, a young family came in to visit: a mother, father, and a boy and a girl — just like the one he had. They reminded Toby so much of Peter, Sandra, Samantha, and Mason. They were even about the same age. The family stopped for a long time in front of Sadie's run with Anne beside them as a guide, always in her funny green boots.

"This girl was found running loose near the ballpark in the East End," Anne told the family. "We were sure someone would come and claim her, as she was definitely someone's dog, but she's been with us for two weeks now and no one has come for her." Anne's voice was warm and kind.

"She's a wonderful looking dog," said the woman, stepping back a pace to get a better look into Sadie's kennel.

The man peered into the run, making soft clicking noises with his tongue. Sadie stood at the gate, wiggling her whole body and gently licking any finger that reached through the fencing.

"Do you want to take her out?" said the man, looking at the wife with a hopeful expression on his face.

The woman stood for a moment and looked at Sadie in the shadows of her cell. A small smile creased her lips and she nodded. Without hesitation, Anne had Sadie out of her kennel on a leash and headed for the door.

Toby moved to the outside area of his kennel and after a few moments, he could see her in the play yard with the young family. She was running at full speed across the play yard, a thing of pure grace. Then she bounced and jumped for tennis balls thrown by the family, her muzzled energy finally unleashed. The young family was clearly pleased with her antics. The children giggled together in one corner of the yard while the husband and wife held hands watching the exuberant young dog and tossing her the ball each time she brought it for them. Toby observed them from a distance. The man and woman seemed fit and healthy, maybe runners like Peter once was. He thought that Sadie would probably enjoy someone to run with.

After a long moment gathering his large frame under his long legs, Jack stood and walked slowly to the fencing beside Toby to see what he was watching. Without making eye contact with Toby, he walked to the back of his enclosure and gazed towards the play yard through large, thoughtful eyes.

"She's really happy to be out there," said Toby. "They really seem to like her — look at their faces, how happy they are."

Jack said nothing and stood in silence, his large shadow blackening the ground of his enclosure. He watched only for a few seconds longer, gave a quiet exhale and walked back into his cell, laying down for a nap.

Toby sat at the edge of his enclosure. He listened and watched intently, thinking of Oscar and how the old dog had survived so long by learning this place. In his mind, Toby began to piece together how things worked here. He understood that these people were coming by to look for a dog to take to the play yard. If a dog went to that play yard and played well, the people were happy. If the people were happy, they may take the dog with them far from this place. And it sure seemed like Sadie was making these people happy. Processing the thoughts and connections, Toby unconsciously let out a squeaky whimper. He wanted to be in the yard making someone happy so that they would take him away too.

Sensing motion next to him, he turned to his left and saw Jack looking out at him, lowering his giant head through the opening in the concrete. He must have been roused by Toby's whimper.

"It's not your turn," he said simply, and his head disappeared back into his cell.

Toby sat on his haunches and watched quietly. Sadie was in the yard for a long time, playing constantly with the family, chasing the ball and running circles around the yard. The smiles never faded from the family; they seemed to enjoy every moment of it.

The man turned, his head lowered microscopically, and his eyebrows raised as if asking an unspoken question. The woman smiled and nodded to him, and they both looked to the children.

"What do you guys think?" said the man, a question seeded with the answer.

In unison, the children responded.

"We want her!!!" yelled the boy.

"Yes!!!" cheered the little girl.

They both began to jump and dance around the play yard, Sadie joining in the play as she darted around them merrily.

The man turned to Anne and smiled. Anne's even composure faded for a moment; an enormous, genuine smile crossed her face. She nodded back at the man.

"OK, let's go get your paperwork done," she said in a cheerful tone as she slipped a leash on Sadie who would have been agreeable with anything at the moment. Toby watched as Anne led them back through the door to the building. The heavy steel door closed with a metallic hitch, and Toby stared at the empty play yard for several long moments. After a while, he passed back through the small opening into his cell to watch for Sadie's return. He wanted to hear all about her time in the play yard. He sat by the fencing, watching for the door to open, and he waited.

And he waited...

And waited...

But Sadie never came back. Toby sat there motionless for a long, long time, but the door never once opened. Eventually, he lay down on the concrete floor and tucked himself into a ball, his eyes still angled to the door should it open for Sadie to come walking through.

Sadie never came back that day. A deep sadness washed over Toby. The realization that Sadie was not coming back slowly sank into his consciousness. Beside him sat her empty kennel, a reminder of their suddenly disparate places in this world. He dipped his head to his paws and closed his eyes once more, his heart sinking for the thousandth time in his young life.

The rest of the day dragged on, and Toby was bogged down in his sorrow. Only a few people came in to look at the dogs. None of them stopped even briefly to give Toby a second look.

As the sun fell outside, Derrick came through the kennel and began pulling at the long wires to close the metal trap doors that blocked off the outer enclosure. Toby was already inside so Derrick didn't have to coax him in. After the realization that Sadie wasn't coming back, Toby had no more desire to go back outside. He just lay inside his cell and moped, his mind often thinking of Marilynn, just feet away, behind the concrete walls. He wished she were here beside him.

The gates closed, and the lights went off. Derrick gave his typically warm "Sweet dreams. See you in the morning" as he closed the door behind him. The kennel grew still and quiet, and Toby settled in on the hard, concrete floor for another long, lonely night.

Morning came harshly as Toby was jolted awake by the sounds of Roland entering. He flung the door open without any sense of subtlety and shuffled quickly down the length of the kennel, bringing with him the stench of foul body odor and a hint of alcohol.

"Rise and shine, doggies!" he bayed. A malignant laugh following the words. He went to the corner where the cleaning supplies were stored and began to unravel the olive-green hose.

Across the kennel, dogs slowly started to rise to their feet. With the sounds of long nails on concrete, the clanking of metal buckles and the occasional rustling of fur as a dog shook the sleep from their minds, everyone was awake. They stood at the edge of their kennels waiting for the inevitable torrent of icy water.

Toby sensed Jack's presence to his right, awake but still laying down.

Roland unwound the hose and set it down in a large curled pile at one end of the kennel. Then he proceeded to the far end, pulling the wire strings attached to pulleys that raised the gates to the outdoor kennels. The man may not have been friendly, but he was quick at his work, and within a few minutes, he had opened the outdoor exits for the 30 kennels in the adoption room and was now back at the hose, turning the valve to full blast.

He started at the far end of the kennel on the opposite end from Toby, spraying indiscriminately into the kennels, pushing the dogs back into their outdoor runs. Food, urine, and feces chased after them in a rush of cold water. All of the dogs were soaked that morning, and Toby was no exception. As Roland came to the front of his cell, he stood defiantly, facing the bitter old man. He had enough of Roland, and as the man approached him with the hose, he began to bark and snap at the fencing, the memories of what Roland had done to Marilynn still fresh in his mind. Roland stood before him and sprayed him square in the snout, the pressure of the water stinging against his skin. Toby withstood the cascade of water, turning his head but continuing to bark. Roland gave another spray, this time squarely to his chest. Toby turned his head towards the man, lowered his brow, and let loose a long deep growl then gnashed at the wire fencing.

Jack stood at the edge of his kennel watching and

listening to the scene unfold. He longed for Toby to stop, to just leave the cell and let Roland do his cleaning. The young dog was doing himself no good, he thought. As the growls, barks, and blasts of water continued in the kennel next door, Jack let loose a deep bark.

"HEY!" he yelled to Toby, hoping to shake the young dog from his furor.

The sound of Jack's bark broke Toby's focus on Roland and redirected his attention. He turned and ducked through the opening in the concrete and loped into the outdoor enclosure, his mind still racing. Jack came through the opening into his enclosure, his brow furrowed, and the sense of passiveness gone. He gave Toby a stern look.

"You're going to make yourself trouble acting like that," he said, his words short and clipped, but the meaning was clear.

Toby laid down on the wet concrete as Roland finished and moved down the line. He was soaked, and his snout and chest hurt. There were small patches of red on his nose where the blasts of water had met the skin beneath his fur.

As the sun rose, the kennel began to dry. Dogs milled in and out of their cells, pacing back and forth to pass the day. The morning was slow with visitors, a few disinterested couples here and there and a handful of young men in their sagging pants who stopped to look at Toby, asking a few questions to Anne as they peered into his cell.

Later in the afternoon, the door opened, and Anne turned the corner, her face wearing a half-smile. Toby could sense that she had a dog with her, but he couldn't yet make out who it was.

"I think you'll be happy to see your buddy," she said, looking downwards at an unseen companion with a broad grin.

And then around the corner strode a familiar golden coat, and Marilynn came into full view at the end of Anne's multi-colored leash. Toby was at the kennel gate in a flash, his whole body wiggling from left to right, his tail countering every wiggle of his body. When Marilynn saw him, she pulled hard on the leash, stretching Anne's slender arm as she rushed towards the kennel. Both dogs jumped up simultaneously on either side of the fencing, their paws on the chain-link. Only the thin wires separated them now. Toby licked furiously at the metal as if he could somehow make his way through with the power of his tongue. Marilynn stepped back and did a little prance, the bright fur on her body shimmering under the fluorescent lights.

"I see you guys remember each other," said Anne sarcastically.

Jack had sauntered up to the front of his kennel as well. He looked for a moment and then, clearly unimpressed, he settled back down on the concrete floor of his cell.

All down the kennel, the other dogs barked at Marilynn. There was Alex, the tiny, funny-looking dog. He was rust and white, seemingly both longer and shorter than he should be with large ears that pointed upwards. His large bark belied his small size, and he made quite a ruckus in his cell. Next to him was Fiona with her short white fur covering a muscled frame. She gave several soft, welcoming barks. Dmitri, the old brown mutt, barked crazily at Marilynn, but he also barked at nothing in particular most of the time. Even the hound dog, Lexi, bayed loudly across the hall.

Anne lifted the chain on Sadie's old kennel, opened the gate, and unclipped the leash, setting Marilynn free inside. Toby started to move and then stutter-stepped, wondering whether to try and greet her again at the front or meet her out back. After a second, he shot through the opening in the concrete to the outside and found her pressed against the chain-link fence. He rose again on his hind paws, scratching at the fencing to get to his friend. After a moment, he settled, and they stood there face to face. Toby stared at her like a goofy love-struck dog. Marilynn stood before him coyly, pretending to look at the concrete but looking longingly at him from the corner of her eye. They were together, and things were right once again.

The days passed like this with Toby and Marilynn side by side across the fencing, rarely even coming forward to meet the visitors unless one of the workers beckoned for them to come in. The visitors were slow those first few days. A few times, various people would stop and look at Marilynn, reaching in to scratch her nose and talking to her softly. On the second day, Derrick came and brought Marilynn out of her kennel, and she walked away with an older woman with wispy silvery hair and a soft gray sweater. Toby watched from the front of his cell.

After the door closed, Toby raced to the backside of his kennel and stared into the play yard, watching for the door to open. After a moment, it did, and Derrick set Marilynn free in the yard. The older woman sat down on the wooden bench and called her. Marilynn was so excited and didn't even hear the call. She ran and ran, circling the yard, her long fur rising horizontally as the air rushed past her. Eventually, she heard the woman's calls and charged towards her at full steam, half jumping as she rapidly approached, landing her torso in the woman's lap. The woman tilted backward, almost falling off the bench as Derrick reached for Marilynn's collar and pulled her off. Toby let out a series of yips, and Marilynn looked from the distance to the sound of the familiar noises.

The old woman laughed as Derrick pulled Marilynn from her lap. She spoke to him. Toby couldn't make out the sounds of her words, but after a moment the leash was back on Marilynn, and Derrick led her back through the door into the shelter. Remembering his last sight of Sadie, Toby let out a deep, panicked bark, realizing he may never see Marilynn again. The pained bark resonated through the kennel, causing the rest of the shelter to go silent. He barked again and again and again, and then he sat motionless in his kennel.

And several long, painful moments later, the door opened, and in came Derrick with Marilynn in tow. Soon she was beside him again just on the other side of the fencing, and the two lay side by side. Her brief departure quickly faded into the bliss between them.

The days came and went. Toby and Marilynn quickly got on the same routine. Their mornings always started with Roland and his menacing hose, but the two dogs learned to hide, pressed back to back in the chain-link area, avoiding the brunt of the cold water in a space just out of reach. When Derrick or Anne would bring treats as they often did, the two dogs would gently carry the treats into the open space and lay quietly, chewing them, never interrupting the other until they each were done. For two straight days, there were no visitors to the shelter, no one came down their rows to stare at them. Toby thought that the shelter must be closed as the workers all quickly cleaned their areas and were gone for the day until someone came back many hours later and brought them in for the evening. It was quieter these two days, and there was some solace in the silence, but Toby grew sad inside. Without any visitors, there was no chance for someone to see him and take him or Marilynn home. He knew Marilynn felt the same, but she seemed to be holding up well.

Towards the end of the second day, a cool wind blew in from the outside and the leaves swirled around the parking lot. The shelter was quiet all day, and Toby and Marilynn enjoyed their time relaxing outside, letting the breeze ruffle their coats until they grew cold and went back to the relative warmth of their concrete cells. Jack stirred around his kennel an unusual amount this day. The old dog seemed aware of something foreign to Toby. Toby tried to make eye contact with him on the few rare occasions when Jack came outdoors, but the big dog always looked away, sniffing the air as if searching for some mysterious scent.

The sound of boots in the hallway beyond the door stirred Toby from a slumber, and he moved towards the front of his gate. From the sounds, he knew it was more than one person. He craned his head and could just barely see out the glass door that led into the main hallway. He could see Derrick and Roland walking side by side and headed for the Holding Area. Toby gave a whimper to Derrick although he knew that the man could not hear him through the metal door. The large man had an unusually somber look on his face as he followed Roland with a leash in his hand. The door to the Holding Area opened and closed behind them, and Toby could no longer see. Next door, Jack puffed a loud, audible sigh.

A long moment passed in silence and then there was clanging: the unmistakable racket of Julius banging his water pail across the concrete. Then Julius began his barking, deep and threatening, almost verging on complete madness. Toby knew that Julius liked Derrick, so the tenor of his barking surprised him. Perhaps it was Roland he was barking at. Then the clanging stopped. There were two more barks, and then it was quiet for several long seconds. Now other barks rose as a chorus from the other dogs in the Holding Area. The loud shouts echoed through the hallway and punctured the very walls of the kennel. Somewhere in that cacophony, Toby recognized a familiar voice — Oscar.

Toby was instantly alarmed. Oscar never barked, but he was now, a deep, afflicted sound rising from somewhere within him. The door opened, and Roland's hand extended, pressing the door against the side of the wall to hold it wide. Derrick passed to his left through the doorway, holding tightly to a short red leash, a sense of profound anguish etched across his face. Toby looked down the leash, just to the edges of the windowed door and saw Julius. He was a filthy sight: his red and white patches were stained with damp grime, his paws raw and swollen. He was skinnier than when Toby last saw him. Julius pulled at the leash and circled feverishly in the hallway as Derrick struggled to control him. Julius spun towards Derrick and jumped, gnashing once at the leash and then dropping to the ground. The barking from the Holding Area poured into the hallway. Oscar's barks were still discernible in the uproar, a panicked sound that Toby had never heard from him before. As the door closed firmly behind the two men, the barks subsided into a dull muffle.

Derrick started down the hall with Julius leading the way erratically. Roland followed close behind. They passed by the window in the door and were gone from sight. Toby sat motionless, trying to make sense of it all. As the moments passed, everything fell quiet again. The raucous noises of stress and dismay faded invariably into the dull monotony.

Toby sat by the front of his cell for a long time waiting for Julius to come back. He wished he could talk to Oscar and find out what was happening. After a long while, Toby heard the boots in the hallway again and waited to see Julius pass the window. Toby pressed against the fencing, looking towards the window in the door. Two pairs of boots indeed passed the window: Derrick and Roland headed back to the Holding Area. Derrick held the red leash in his hand, but this time, there was no one at the end.

Toby grew anxious and concerned, shuffling his feet in his kennel. The door to the Holding Area closed again and the men disappeared. Once again, the discordant barking began anew. Toby shivered in his cell as Marilynn and Jack stood motionless on either side of him. There was only silence in the Adoption Area as everyone sensed something grave was happening across the hall.

One long, slow minute passed, and then two. Finally, the door to the Holding Area opened a second time as Roland once again reached his wiry arm around and braced the door. Out came Derrick, holding the red leash. Toby's eyes followed the bright leash to the floor again. His heart dropped as he saw Oscar at the end, the old, brown dog walking slowly. He seemed tired but not defeated. He looked like a dog who had always known this day would come.

As Oscar crossed the threshold of the door, he lifted his head. His single eye shone proudly, as proud as Toby could ever recall. Oscar turned his head with purpose and looked into the Adoption Area. For a brief second, their eyes connected once more through the dusty window. All of the wisdom Oscar had imparted to Toby came rushing back like a tidal wave. He knew now with a deep sadness why Oscar had shared so much. He had given Toby a chance, a chance to get out of this place and to be free from these walls. He knew right then that Oscar had always been doomed, that he would never know a family of his own, never enjoy the comfort of a soft plush bed, or taste the sweet pure air of the outdoors. But through Toby, Oscar could be free.

The weight of the emotions rushed through Toby in the instant it took for the two to lock eyes, the clarity of this world coming at him suddenly. Oscar raised his head slightly, the captain of his fate. Then he turned and marched down the hall.

As their gaze broke, Toby let out a shrill whine that pierced the air like a knife. His paws raked up and down on the chain-link fence, trying desperately to break through to his friend. But he could not. The little dog scratched and clawed until his feet were raw, long after Oscar, Derrick, and Roland had disappeared from sight. Jack and Marilynn did nothing, standing mute on either side of him.

After many minutes passed, Toby slid his front paws down the fencing and dropped to all fours. Once more, he flopped to the concrete, his eyes blank and lifeless, and he lay there, a tide of dark desolation sweeping over him. How many times would his heart break, he wondered?

High in the rafters above him, the little wren looked on, his tiny domed head tilted sideways in thoughtful observance. Suddenly, his wings flittered quickly, and he dove through another small gap in the vent to the blue sky beyond, leaving the caged souls behind.

# CHAPTER 10

The days that followed were hard on Toby. The realization of what had become of Oscar and Julius dawned on him and sank deep into his soul, resting heavily like a stone on his heart. The innocent optimism that there was some way out of this place began to fade, the space filled with the boredom and frustration of his confinement.

Even Derrick drew his ire. Once viewed as a friend, Toby now viewed the large, dreadlocked man only as the one who killed Oscar and Julius. Toby would not let Derrick close to the kennel any longer. When he came to water the dogs or deliver food, Toby would bare his teeth, lean back on his haunches and give a stern growl. Derrick would usually fill the water bowl quickly with the green pitcher and leave, but every now and then he would sit on the concrete floor, ignoring Toby's display of aggression and talk to him softly. The words meant nothing to Toby, but they were kind and delicate in their manner. None of them mattered, though. Derrick had taken Oscar away, and *that* is the only thing that mattered.

While Toby was outwardly frustrated at Derrick, he displaced the affection towards Anne, and their bond grew over the days after Oscar and Julius' passing. The slender young woman with the dark ponytail sensed Toby's growing tension in the shelter and would make special efforts to spend a long time with him whenever she could. The two often visited the play yard where Anne would throw Toby the ball and yell encouragement at him to give chase. Toby had little interest, or perhaps energy, to chase. It seemed that he had aged tremendously in his short time here. He was no longer bouncing and energetic and only milled around the play yard sniffing the fence and the trailing scents of the other dogs. Anne would sit on the bench and call for him. Occasionally, he would come, and when he did she would cradle his head in her hands and massage his forehead, whispering gently to him that everything would be alright.

Every so often, Toby was let out in the play yard with Marilynn. In these times, his true spirit could not be suppressed despite the negativity that surrounded him. The two dogs remained inseparable, running and jumping at each other, free from the worries of the kennel, the troubled scents, the loud noises, and the general despair of the place. Marilynn was remarkably well composed and was holding up well in the shelter. She was quick to play, always perking up instantly once brought from her kennel. Marilynn was fond of all of the workers, and they very much felt the same of her.

These scant times with Marilynn in the yard were the only bright spots in Toby's life now. Even when young Katie, a teenage volunteer at the shelter, would give Toby a special peanut butter-filled rubber toy, the sadness of the place overshadowed any happiness he might otherwise find in the savory treat. It was only Marilynn who could lift his spirits now.

Over the course of the next week, dogs came and went from the Adoption Area. There was a new dog just above Toby now. His name was Dizzy Dean, and he looked like a tiny version of Toby's mother: stout and white but with a bright pink nose. The funny little dog would run in circles and spin around, chasing his tail. He provided the kennel with a general sense of comedic relief and everyone seemed amused by his good-natured antics. While Toby couldn't see him from below, he would see the little dog as he came and went to the play yard and could hear him circling above. And Dizzy Dean always let Toby know that he was there with his occasional, chipper barks.

Jack was still in the kennel beside Toby, passing time as Jack did: silently and stoically. Toby would see him on occasion when Anne or Melissa would take him for a walk. The fur was now worn from his joints which now appeared pale and reddish, the product of many days passed on the hard, concrete floor. Through it all, though, Jack remained passive and unaffected. Toby had never seen another dog like this one, so unmoved by the world around him. He wondered if that was why Jack had been here for so long. Dmitri had told him one day that the big brown dog had been in that same kennel for eight long months now, and not one person had come to adopt him. Toby grew sad at this news. How long would he wait for a home of his own? Or would he end up like Oscar and Julius?

The second week after Oscar and Julius passed went just as slowly as the first. The weather was getting colder now as winter was on its way. The formerly cool wind from outside became icy and frigid, often reducing Toby and Marilynn's play times to a fraction of what they had once been.

Over that week, Toby thought often about Oscar and Julius and wondered what exactly had happened to them. The sadness in Jack's eyes told him all the details he needed to know, yet he still wondered. Toby hoped the two were at peace now. Perhaps they had found solitude far away from this cold, concrete shelter. Maybe somewhere up in the blue sky, far away where the little wren flies, Julius no longer needed to clank his metal bowl, and his troubled mind was finally at peace.

Marilynn's spirits were unflappable as the weeks passed. Nothing seemed to phase her, her soul well-armored against the dark moments that surrounded them. Her demeanor particularly impressed the staff who praised her in high-pitched tones whenever they passed by to fill the water bowls or offer treats.

As the days went on, Toby's resentment of Derrick slowly subsided as the big, kind man continued with patience and warmth in his daily routine, unaltered by

Toby's aggressions. He paid extra special attention to Toby these days. Even when the young black dog was barking and growling at the front of his kennel, Derrick never once raised his voice or admonished him. His calm demeanor wore down the anger like a determined river over a jagged stone, and after some time Toby couldn't help but warm to him again.

In steady contrast to Derrick's kindness, Roland continued his morning fusillade of cold water. One time Anne caught him spraying in Dizzy's kennel and yelled at him, stomping towards him angrily in her green boots and admonishing the older man with tones none of the dogs had ever heard from her before. Roland had ducked his head sheepishly and muttered something incomprehensible to both dog and man. Anne had taken the hose from him and showed him how to spray properly. She showed him how to let the dog out the back and into cover and how to avoid spraying debris and feces onto the dogs. None of it did any good, though. The next day, Roland was back to his antics, blasting cold water on the dogs as they stood outside in the early winter morning.

The long fur of Marilynn's coat held a great deal of water, and Toby wished more than anything that he could be beside her to help dry her off or somehow warm her with the heat from his body. Every morning, he would press himself firmly against the chain-link and slide his body along the length of his outdoor enclosure, squeezing the moisture from his fur. When he finished, he would move closer to Marilynn as she shook and licked herself, somehow hoping that his proximity would warm her.

One particular afternoon, there was an assortment of people through the kennel, pacing the aisle and staring occasionally into the kennels. As usual, no one had expressed any interest in Toby. In fact, most people gave nothing more than a glance at the shadowy creature tucked in the back of his kennel. Jack invariably attracted some "Awwww"s and sighs of empathy as the big dog was almost too large for his kennel, his large worn frame presenting something of a pathetic image to the passers-by.

A couple of people, including a middle-aged man and a younger woman, had separately stopped and admired Marilynn, spending long minutes transfixed on her smiling face and her lavish coat of golden fur. The young woman even had Melissa take her out, and Toby watched, fixated on the play yard as the woman smiled widely and Marilynn played casually with a bright green tennis ball. To Toby's relief, Marilynn came back to her cell that day.

But the next day, the young woman was back at the shelter. Toby saw her in the play yard with another dog, a dog that he did not recognize from the shelter. Perhaps she had brought her own dog? Derrick had come and brought Marilynn out to meet with the woman and this new dog. Marilynn was confident and happy, as she always was, but the woman's dog, a small and wiry terrier, growled and snapped at Marilynn, pulling taut at the end of its leash. And before long, Marilynn was back again beside Toby, both unaware at how close she had been to finding a home of her own.

The following day, Toby learned how to push back a section of wire dividing his kennel from Marilynn's just enough to squeeze his paw through. Marilynn would lay next to the open space, and Toby would reach through, his paw resting gently next to hers, the most he could manage through the tiny gap in the wire. The two dogs sat like this for hour after hour, the cold wind causing all of the other dogs to seek shelter in their concrete kennels. Jack would occasionally poke his head out to watch the two laying on the cold concrete, heads down and paws crossed. After a glance, he would dip his head and duck back under into the concrete opening, indifferent as always.

A few days later, the kennel was full of a great many people. The weather had taken a turn for the better, and the sun shone in the crisp blue sky. Several people stopped to look at Marilynn, and on more than one occasion, she was taken to the play yard to visit. Each time, Toby's heart dropped; he was never sure if she would return. Toby didn't like any of the people who took Marilynn out, and he was relieved when she would return every time.

The following day, an older couple came to visit. Toby sensed immediately that the man had a kindly glow about him; his face was warm with wise wrinkles. A pair of black-framed glasses rested on the edge of his nose, and his hair was a speckle of gray and white. He wore an old, comfortable wool sweater and shuffled slightly as he walked. The woman gave off the same kindly aura. Their two spirits seemed strangely intertwined as one. Her cheeks were rosy and pudgy, her smile genuine and wide, and she wore an old dotted dress that looked like it came from another time. When words came from her mouth, it called to Toby. It seemed to call to all of the dogs as they gathered at the edges of their cells, entranced in the serenity of her voice. It was unmistakably the voice of someone who knew and loved dogs.

As the couple walked up and down the kennel with Anne leading the way, they stopped at every run, leaning in and talking gently to the dogs. They never passed a kennel without stopping to acknowledge the occupants. Even the ragged mutt Dmitri was greeted with kindness. When they approached Lexi, the hound began to bay incessantly. While most visitors walked away at the sounds, the woman merely stood there, smiling. "Ohhhhhh, aren't you a special one?" she said, doting on the noisy hound.

As they moved down the aisle, they came to Marilynn's cage and leaned in close, both of them side by side admiring her. Toby shuffled to the edge of his kennel, and the man saw him out of the corner of his eye and gave him a soft smile, reaching his fingers through to scratch Toby on the snout. Toby dipped his head to meet the fingers, and the man continued, but his attention was mostly on Marilynn.

"She's a great dog," said Anne. "Someone's family

pet, for sure. She's only been here a few weeks but is holding up very well."

The older couple spoke for a while with Anne, asking a few questions and listening intently to Anne's responses. They never took their gaze off of Marilynn though. In turn, she sat at attention before them, panting softly.

"We'd like to take her out to see," said the man pleasantly. He smiled and looked at his wife, who smiled back. Anne grinned slightly and nodded then walked towards the end of the aisle and retrieved a leash from the metal hook. She opened the kennel, attached the leash to Marilynn's collar, and Marilynn strode out confidently. She paused at Toby's kennel and stepped forward to press her nose flush against the wire. Toby whimpered and pressed forward as well. Through the fencing, he could feel her soft tongue lick the edge of his snout. The feeling warmed him to his core. She looked at him for a moment and her eyes were bright and filled with hope.

Anne gave a soft tug on the leash. Marilynn held Toby's eyes for just a second longer, then turned and followed the older couple across through the door. There was a sense of finality in her departure, and Toby could feel that this time it was for real.

# CHAPTER 11

The world changed once Marilynn was gone. Toby had been through a lot, but nothing felt quite like this. Not the passing of Oscar and Julius. Not the move from his home with the family to the shelter. Not even leaving his mother in the backyard. This was somehow different.

He had been in this place less than four weeks and had known Marilynn for most of that time. The bond between them, forged in the darkness of their shared condition, had been even more powerful than he had realized… until now. The prospect to see Marilynn, to spend time with her across the wire, to frolic and play with her in the play yard, had buoyed his sagging spirits and helped push the cold dread of this place to the farthest corners of his mind. He had something to clutch onto and keep him adrift, something to keep the madness at bay and prevent him from spiraling downward like poor Julius.

Anne sensed the turmoil in Toby and had been especially kind that day. She made a point to bring Marilynn back to the kennel to see him after the older couple had decided to adopt her. Anne's face was lined with conflicting emotions of this moment: her joy for Marilynn was tempered with the heartache for Toby. In her best, desperate attempt, she had mentioned coyly to the older couple that Toby was Marilynn's best friend and the two were inseparable. They simply smiled and nodded, assuring her they had only room for one dog, but they promised to mention him to all of their friends.

Anne knew that Toby would never see Marilynn again.

Separations like this were one of the sad, necessary duties of her job at the shelter, but Anne handled it with dignity and compassion as she always did. She let the two dogs sniff and lick enthusiastically through the fencing for several long minutes. The rest of the kennel stood in hushed silence, paying reverence to the moment between them. Marilynn exuded a profound sense of sadness, but just beneath, in the well of her emotions, stirred a great sense of optimism for both herself and for Toby.

She stepped back a pace and stood facing him, the two separated only by the thin steel wires. Toby's paws slid down from the fencing, and he grew still, his eyes fixated on her angular face.

"I believe in you, Toby," Marilynn said.

Anne watched the moment from the end of the leash, aware only that the two dogs were communicating in ways that humans could never fully appreciate. Tears welled in her eyes and ran down her cheeks, leaving dark stains on her smock. She gave a gentle tug on the leash. Marilynn paused and lingered a moment longer in front of Toby's cell, her eyes full of hope. Then they turned and walked out the door.

Toby sank to the concrete floor and lay there silently. After a moment, a motion to his right stirred him from his stupor and he turned his head to look. Next to him, stretched out under the wire and angled towards him was a single, large, brown paw. It was Jack. Toby rested his head on the concrete and closed his eyes, longing for the blackness to engulf him and set him free of this place.

The next two days were a foggy haze. Toby had no energy, no appetite, and no emotion. When they brought him food, he barely moved and only nibbled occasionally. Even the icy water from Roland's hose could not stir him to life and eventually, the scraggly old man felt sorry for him and began to spray around him.

In those few days, Derrick and Anne would come more regularly, often bringing Toby new toys and treats. They worked hard to keep his spirits up. Toby wasn't interested in any of the treats and only occasionally sampled them, most of the time taking a bite or two and then dropping the remainder on the concrete floor before him where it remained for the rest of the day.

Anne and Derrick talked about what to do and decided to put Dizzy beside him in Marilynn's old kennel. They hoped that the silly little dog might help revive Toby's sagging spirits. It didn't work. Dizzy would spin and spin, scratching at the chain-link, pleading with Toby to play but to no avail.

The next three weeks passed like this. Toby spent the majority of his time in the dark corners of his cell curled into a ball, huddled in the comforting shadows.

During this time, there was one small, bright spot as a new volunteer began to visit the sad, young dog. With her long blonde hair, lively gait, and perpetually cheerful tone, Allison, a young student at a nearby college, was instantly liked by all of the residents in the Adoption Area. She had never volunteered with animals before and was new to the shelter. In the innocence of her young mind, every visit was a step towards making the world right by these forsaken animals.

On her first visit to the shelter, she seemed immediately drawn to Toby. As the door opened, she strode directly towards his kennel. Toby heard the door swing open and saw a strange new person heading towards him. He lifted his head to catch her scent. While all of the visitors carried with them the familiar scents of cleaning chemicals or other animals, Toby sensed something different in the girl. His nostrils flared and closed as a million invisible particles began to help Toby understand.

She walked carefully and quietly to the front of his kennel and stood for a moment, and then she crouched slowly and sat down on the concrete floor before him. Most of the strange people who came to the Adoption

Area glanced into the darkened alcove only for a moment and then passed on, the fuzzy shape of a black dog melding with the shadows and not capturing their interest. But this girl was different, he thought.

Allison sat for a long time on the concrete, talking softly to Toby as he watched her, only his head moving subtly to follow her movements. After several minutes, she lifted her slight hand and placed it against the fencing for him to smell. Toby paused for a moment, and then leaned forward, capturing her scents. Several more minutes passed and then she opened the gate between them. He could see her now, unobscured by the steel wires. She was smiling at him, unthreatening and unassuming. She reached forward slowly and rested her hand on the side of his neck and began to stroke his dusty fur. Then she beckoned him forward with her hands, the leash dangling before him. Guided by her warmth, he gathered his legs and stood, then took two steps, and he was before her. She rubbed the back of his neck as she clipped on the leash and led him out the door.

It had been a long time since Toby had been outside of the building. He felt dirty and ashamed of the way he looked. As they passed the tall front desk in the lobby, Toby could see Anne and Derrick looking at him. They each rose from their chairs and gave a wide smile, their joy clear but unspoken.

As they walked, Allison spoke to Toby softly the whole time, encouraging him forward. When they reached the grass, he crouched and urinated for a long minute. He scratched his rear feet vigorously in the dirt where he had marked, letting the world know he had been here. Allison laughed innocently at his antics.

They walked a short while, and Allison stopped at a wide, plastic bench before a neighboring building. She sat and gestured for Toby to come to her lap. Toby cocked his head, unsure of the gesture, but then reared on his back legs and placed his paws and head in her lap. Her long, blonde hair draped across the back of his neck as she leaned forward and pressed her body against him in a great hug. He felt invigorated at this moment as the cool, crisp wind ruffled the fur on his back and he sank into the depth of Allison's embrace.

After a while, they rose and walked some more. Toby wished that the walk would never end. But as they rounded the last corner, he saw the shelter before him and froze, his body trembling. Allison turned and looked, realizing the gravity of the moment. She made a playful running start to encourage him forward, but he would not move. He simply hunkered down until she had to lift him to all fours and coax him to walk. His pace was slow and unsteady. When they reached the shelter door, he sank again to the ground, cloaking the "Welcome" mat with his trembling form.

Allison bent down and spoke softly to him. For a long while, he did not move. Visitors came and went through the door for the next several minutes, many casting a sympathetic glance at the young dog and the young girl. She sat beside him for quite some time before finally lifting him up and carrying him through the doors and back to his kennel. Toby sat absorbed in grief. The walk with Allison and the comfort she had shown had momentarily mended his wounded heart, but his re-entry to this place now clung to him like a tremendous weight. Allison sat with him for some time in his cell, her head tucked low under the concrete and her whole body curled into the small space. After some time, she rose, stroked the base of his neck, and closed the gate. She turned and walked away down the aisle, pausing to look back at him with a sad expression as she hung the leash from a metal hook and left.

Time crept along slowly. Each day that followed seemed interminable and even longer than the day before. The noises of the kennel were amplified now, sinking deeply and maddeningly into Toby's consciousness. Allison's regular visits were a welcome reprieve, but they were fleeting and temporary. At the end, the kennel always awaited him.

Jack took notice of the sinking spirits of the young dog beside him. The big dog would often sit outside in the fenced enclosure behind his cell, looking diagonally through the fence into Toby's cell, keeping vigil on the huddled mass. Many times, the cold winds and rain weren't enough to drive Jack back into his cell. There wasn't much he could do, but even the big, stoic dog knew how important it was for Toby to feel like someone was there for him.

Next door, Dizzy continued to spin and jump in his kennel, seemingly unbothered by Toby's lack of participation. Every now and then, Dizzy would yip at

Toby as if the random sound would rouse the dog. It never did. Only occasionally would Toby leave his cell to pace in the fenced enclosure, rarely interacting with Dizzy or Jack on either side of him. For the remainder of the time, he lay curled against the concrete wall, motionless and alone.

"He's not doing well at all. We have to do something," said Anne to the short, stout, gray-haired woman named Susan who oversaw the shelter. The look of urgency was clear on Anne's face.

They both looked at him curled in the darkness. A mix of thoughtfulness and concern blanketed their faces.

"What if we move him to the end where he's closer to everyone coming and going?" asked Susan in her funny twang, pointing to the far end of the hallway.

"He has something of a bond with Jack, I think. I think moving him away might hurt even more," replied Anne, glancing back and forth between Toby and Jack.

"You're probably right," responded Susan, her stubby hand caressing her round chin.

Anne looked over at Dizzy and smiled. "Dizzy, you were supposed to cheer him up. You didn't do a very good job," she said playfully, reaching in to pet the white dog who pawed at the kennel in oblivious delight. "Would you mind if I took him home for a few nights?" said Anne, seemingly out-of-the-blue.

Susan looked surprised and shook her head vigorously "Of course not. If you think you can manage it. I bet it would do him a lot of good."

"We'll see how it goes," Anne replied, a slight hint of concern in her voice. "I'll take him for a bit and see what happens."

# CHAPTER 12

The soft carpet felt strange and foreign on Toby's dull, cracked pads. The last time he had felt carpet on his feet was many months ago inside the house of his former family — before he had been cast to the backyard, before he ended up at the shelter. The carpet was soft and springy, and it tickled the fur between his toes as he walked. Toby liked this new sensation.

Anne closed the door behind him quietly and let go of his leash, and Toby stood completely still for a brief moment, processing the smells and sounds of the small apartment. The residue of cooked food from many hours earlier crept into Toby's nasal passages, mixing with the scent of a fragrant candle, the aroma of an air freshener plugged into the wall, and the distinctive smell of another dog. He stood and took in all of the scents, filtering through them with his twitching nose and whiskers.

Behind a door to his left, he heard a scratching noise and a whimpering. It sounded like an older dog, and from the smell he could tell it was a male dog.

"Brutus, settle down," said Anne, her voice reflecting a mighty bond with the dog behind the door.

Toby took several small steps forward into the tiny living room. He noticed a large dog bed beside the television and crept towards it, his nose inhaling all of its smells. After that, he crept towards the sofa, sniffing under the coffee table on the way. He made his way to the kitchen and smelled at the closed cabinets, then to a tiny bedroom where his nose drew him to a half-stuffed toy in the shape of some woodland creature. Finally, he nosed into the bathroom but turned back, the narrow walls reminding him of the confines of his cell. In the span of several minutes, Toby had explored the whole space of the small apartment except for the room with the closed door, the one with Brutus behind it.

"What do you think, buddy? You want to stay here for a few days? Maybe get you out of the funk you're in?" said Anne, seated now on the sofa gazing at him. He was uncertain of the look she gave. Her tone was upbeat and happy, but in the lines of her face, he thought he sensed a hint of sorrow.

Toby looked at her and listened, focusing now on her gentle words. As she spoke, his tail wagged a long, slow arc back and forth and back and forth. This place was much better than the shelter. It smelled comfortable, lived in, and happy. Toby liked it here. He felt more relaxed and thought that perhaps he could find a part of his old self here. Another whimper came from the other side of the door, interrupting Toby's thoughts.

152

Anne turned, her shoulders facing the closed door. "Alright, Brutus, are you ready to come and meet Toby?" she asked through the door. She stood and came to Toby, clipping a leash to his collar. In three long steps, she was across the room of the tiny apartment, holding the leash in one hand while gently turning the door handle with the other.

Out of the darkened room, crouching and tail wagging like some happily crazed mongrel came a tall, lanky, brindle-colored dog. His ears were pinned back, and his tail wagged frenetically. He was longer and taller than Toby, but skinny and strange in figure. Toby thought he gave off a funny vibe, like a clownish dog, even goofier and crazier than Dizzy.

Brutus sniffed quickly around Toby, spastically altering sniffs with play bows and sudden gyrations as if he had already started to play by himself. Toby stood patiently, mostly perplexed at this odd creature before him. Then after a moment, he lowered into a quick play bow, then immediately stood tall again, placing his face just inches from Brutus' ear. His tail wagged slowly as if it was a metronome counting the seconds until the skinny dog would play. Brutus took the bait and darted across the room, propelling himself across the spongy carpet with sinewy legs. Toby pulled hard on the leash and went after him, his body wiggling with excitement from nose to tail. Anne held firm for a moment, then dropped the leash and the two dogs chased each other through the apartment, knocking furniture and knick-knacks asunder as they went.

Anne sat down on the couch; the well-worn cushions sank deeply below her tiny frame. She smiled broadly to herself as she watched Toby and Brutus play, this time without an ounce of sorrow. The two dogs played until they were exhausted. Eventually, they curled beside each other on a large, worn dog bed and fell asleep.

The next morning, Anne woke early and took the dogs out for a bathroom break. They had worn themselves out the night prior and both dogs were slow to wake, but once aroused, they seemed more than happy to trounce side by side down the steps of the apartment building and out into the morning sun.

Toby seemed rejuvenated. A single night out of the shelter brought brightness to his eyes that Anne had not seen for a very long time. Even his gait carried a renewed confidence, a confidence injected with the vibrancy of his new, fast friend. Anne noticed that Brutus seemed more alive also, seemingly quite pleased to have the young dog as company in his tiny, little home.

After a morning routine, Anne packed Toby into the vehicle and headed to work. Unfortunately, Toby would have to spend the day back in the kennel while she worked and then she would bring him back home again that night. Anne thought that last night went better and had done more good for Toby than she expected. She was initially worried that Brutus might overwhelm Toby but was suddenly optimistic that she might be able to foster Toby for an extended period of time. She knew that was the best way to break through his depression.

Toby hedged when they pulled up at the shelter. He gave a whimper that Anne painfully interpreted as a realization of betrayal. He leaned backward, sinking firmly into the rear seat, his haunches pressed deep into the cloth. It took Anne several minutes to coax him out, and as she led him through the doorway, she could physically see the anxiety and sadness creeping back into his body. She spoke to him the whole walk to his kennel, her tone overly cheery and upbeat. As Toby entered his cell and hunkered down in his familiar corner against the concrete, Anne couldn't help but feel that even huddled as he was, there was still a tiny, bright spark in him that wasn't there before. She thought that was a good sign and was hopeful that several more days may do wonders for his prospects of adoption.

Jack sauntered to the front of his cell and pressed his big, black nose against the wire. He gave three long snuffs as if to confirm it was Toby who had been placed back beside him. Satisfied, he turned stoically and curled most of his large frame on the plastic platform that served as his bed. Anne watched him, quietly, thinking to herself that old Jack would never show it, but he seemed happy to know that Toby was still around.

In contrast, on the other side of Toby, Dizzy was expectedly ecstatic. He jumped and barked at the chain-link that divided their kennels and darted from inside to outside several times, hoping to draw Toby to come to the fence and play. Toby couldn't resist the raucous anymore, so he stood and slowly walked through the concrete opening. He pressed his nose against the fence to greet the happy little dog.

"It's so good to see you, Toby!" said Dizzy, the words rushing forth as if they had been bottled up for days.

"Hello, Dizzy," replied Toby. His words were slow, but the glimmer of geniality was unmistakable below the surface.

The day passed uneventfully in the shelter. Several visitors came and went, including: a mother and her small children looking for a toy dog; a gruff, older man looking for his lost pit bull; a young college couple in search of their first dog; and a lonely, middle-aged man looking for a nothing more than a companion. The latter found his match in Zeke, an older black dog with a white muzzle who barely made a peep down at the far end of the kennel. Toby had watched Zeke and the man in the play yard and could tell right away that they were a good match; their energies seemed similar. He didn't know Zeke well as his kennel was so far away, but he felt a great sense of happiness for the old dog as he watched him bounce a tennis ball with his paws and push it towards the man. The slouched man picked it up and threw it weakly, the ball traveling only a few feet. But it was far enough for Zeke, who loped along after it and returned it to the man who stood beaming, suddenly seeming taller and prouder than before.

The day felt somehow different, as in his heart

Toby could sense that he would go home with Anne again. There was just no way that the fun he experienced with Brutus last night was temporary. At the times when he saw Anne throughout the day, she seemed somewhat nervous, but there was no sense of the deep sadness that he had felt in people before like he had with Derrick after Oscar and Julius were gone.

At the end of the day, Anne came back into the kennels after all the wires had been pulled and the doors had shut on their outdoor enclosures. She walked to Toby's kennel in her tall, green boots.

"Are you ready to go, bubby?" she said, looking towards him as she approached.

Toby let out a happy whimper and was at the edge of his kennel before Anne was even halfway there. She opened the gate, clipped on the leash, and away they went as she whispered "goodbyes" to the rest of the dogs on their way out the door.

The ride home seemed to take no time as Toby's mind was occupied with thoughts of another romp with Brutus. As they entered the apartment, Brutus rushed forward to greet him, ignoring Anne and flying into a fit of licks and sniffs. The lanky, brindle dog was all legs and elbows as he bounced around the room imploring Toby to chase him. He didn't have to ask twice, as Toby quickly took to the chase. The two dogs played for just a few minutes before Anne separated them, leashed them up, and took them outside.

After a short walk around the perimeter of her apartment complex, Anne decided to stop by her mailbox in the common area before returning inside. Opening the slot with her key, she was surprised to find a single piece of mail in a plain white envelope. Turning it over, she saw the name of her apartment complex, Sheridan Crossing Apartments. Her stomach sank. With her meager paycheck from the shelter, Anne lived day-to-day, and she immediately grew concerned that her rent check must have bounced.

She flipped the envelope back over and opened it; it wasn't even sealed. Pulling out a one-page letter, she began to read, unconsciously holding her breath.

*Apartment 103*
*Tenant: Anne Kersey*

*Ms. Kersey,*
*It has been brought to our attention that you currently have in your apartment a second dog that is not currently on your lease agreement. In addition to this violation of your lease terms as it relates to the number of dogs in your apartment, the dog in question is a breed that is prohibited on our property. Please refer to Section IV, Article 12 of your lease agreement entitled "Aggressive Animals."*

*You have until Friday, October 21st at 8:00AM to remove this dog from your property. Failure to remove the dog from the property will result in the initiation of eviction proceedings.*

*Sincerely,*

# CHASING THE BLUE SKY

*Katherine J. Bootz*
*Sheridan Crossing Apartments – Leasing Manager*

Anne leaned back against the wall and her tiny frame slid down the brick until she was slumped on the concrete of the entryway. The letter hung loosely in her hand. Brutus and Toby watched her slink downwards and thought it must be a game. They began licking furiously at her face and pawed at the paper to get her to react.

Anne was completely devastated; Toby could not stay with her any longer. She would be evicted, and she had nowhere to go; she had no money to move elsewhere. The unexpected and troubling realization that Toby would have to go back to the shelter engulfed her, and she couldn't help but feel that she had failed him.

She lowered her head and placed it in her small hands and began to cry, the tears rolling unabated down her face. Toby and Brutus sensed now that something was wrong, and they crowded around her, pressing their faces through her hands, trying to break her from her sadness. The words of the letter replayed through Anne's mind. It was so unfair to Toby, she thought. He was not an "aggressive animal." They didn't even know him. They didn't know what he had been through.

She sat there crying for several long minutes, alone in her thoughts. Finally, she composed herself and rose from the ground, ensuring she still had each leash

159

around her wrist.

"Come on guys," she said, the words quiet and broken.

She climbed the stairs with the two happy dogs in tow and entered the tiny apartment. After she got the dogs unleashed and settled in the living room with a pair of treat-stuffed rubber toys, she sat down at the worn old table in the kitchen and began thumbing through a folder to find a number for the rental office. Picking up the phone, she dialed the number and waited for the voicemail. As the phone rang, she reminded herself to be polite and cordial, but as she spoke into the recording, she could hear the resentment in her tone as she explained her receipt of the letter and asked for the manager to call her first thing in the morning.

Toby slept peacefully that night, mostly oblivious to the extent of the turmoil surrounding him. He was content to live in the present, relishing in Anne's affection, the quietness of this new place, and the companionship of his friend, Brutus.

In the morning, Anne woke the dogs and took them outside to the bathroom. Even such mundane activities were exciting for the two dogs, the newness of their interactions painting everything with a happy shade. After they had finished, Anne took Brutus back to the apartment and left for work with Toby once again in the back seat.

Unlike the day before, Toby popped back in the kennel this time, confident that his stay was only temporary. He even stopped briefly at Jack's kennel to let him know he was back and quickly ran to the outdoor enclosure to give greetings to Dizzy who was once again ecstatic at his arrival.

As Anne was walking out of the Adoptions Area, she passed Derrick headed down the other hall. He stopped in his tracks as he passed, grabbed her shoulder gently and spoke.

"What's wrong, girl?" he said as she dipped her head and shook it once as if to say, "Not here."

As the door closed behind her, she walked down the hall out of view of the windowed door. She opened up to Derrick and told him all about the letter and what it meant for Toby. His shoulders visibly slumped at the news as her words sank in. He stood looking dejected for a moment as Anne finished her story.

Before she had finished though, his mood changed and his body seemed to fill with a sudden energy and optimism. He placed one hand on each of her shoulders, squaring her to him, looked her straight in the eye and spoke. "We're going to work on that dog, Anne," he reassured her, his eyes wide and determined. "Break him out of his slump. What you've done has been good, but we've got more to do here," he continued, the confidence building in his voice. Anne, grateful for any sliver of hope, clung to his words, despite a deep uncertainty that they could help the struggling dog and a sense that even Derrick didn't believe what he said.

Toby spent the rest of the day in his kennel, his

mood gradually reviving from the time in Anne's apartment. There were a handful of visitors that day including one neatly dressed young man particularly interested in Dizzy. Dizzy was oblivious to any interest; his antics were the same whether met at his fence with a friendly face or an entirely apathetic one. The young man in his button-up shirt and tan pants smiled curiously as he gazed into the kennel, appearing to appreciate the effusiveness of the little white dog. Soon, Dizzy, Melissa, and the man were in the play yard with the man throwing the bright yellow ball endlessly to Dizzy who returned it over and over and over again until the saliva ran from his jowls.

After a long time, Dizzy returned to the kennel, happy and slobbering. Melissa brought him back to his kennel with the man following close behind. As she closed the gate, the man leaned in and scratched Dizzy under his chin, telling him he would be back. Dizzy, once again unaware of what was said, pranced around then sloppily lapped water from his metal bowl.

As the sun fell in the sky above the play yard, Toby grew more and more anxious to go home with Anne to see Brutus and the small apartment. When Derrick came around to close the outdoor kennel latches, Toby greeted him at the gate, telling with only his eyes that he was ready to go. Derrick only gave a short glance and a half-smile, and it seemed to Toby that he hadn't wanted to look at him. Undeterred, he stood tall at the gate, tail wagging for several long minutes until the door opened again and Anne entered, her head bowed and something in her hand.

Toby's butt moved side to side in anticipation as Anne approached his kennel, the excitement of his impending freedom building within him. As she drew closer, he caught the scent of treats in her hand which was unexpected. Then he sensed the sadness about her as her rubber boots scraped the concrete with an uncharacteristic shuffle. The wag of his tail slowed and then stopped.

She knelt down in front of him and raised her head, her eyes were red, and her mouth was turned downward. Toby whimpered then scratched once at the bottom of the metal gate. Anne reached out and slipped a large, meaty treat through the chain-link. Toby sniffed it and then pushed it away with his paw, still focused on Anne's face.

"I'm so sorry, Toby," she said, the words fading to a near whisper as they left her mouth. "I can't take you home anymore," she continued, dipping her head once more and wiping her nose on her sleeve.

Toby didn't understand the words she said, but her emotion was unmistakable. He sat back on his haunches, processing the scene. Anne leaned forward and slid another treat through the fence, holding it there, but he did not react. Toby stared at her, unblinking, the sounds of Dizzy at his fence whimpering for a treat of his own unheard in the deafening stillness of the moment.

"I'm sorry, buddy," she said again, this time reaching two fingers through the fence, barely able to reach his snout. She dug in her pocket once more and retrieved two more of the meaty treats. She slid them under his gate, rose and walked away. As she reached the door, she flipped the black switch on the wall and left. The halogen lights flickered and went dim as the kennel grew quiet and black.

# CHAPTER 13

T he days that followed passed drearily. Toby lay in his cell and most times wouldn't rise to greet visitors who passed down the aisle. Anne and Derrick made extra efforts to take him out to the play yard, hoping to revive his spirits. On many days, they would alternate coming to work early and leaving late, just to give Toby some extra time outside the building. Allison the volunteer still visited with him regularly, sitting in the tiny concrete space and stroking the length of his fur. All of their extra efforts made little noticeable difference.

While Jack and Dizzy remained next door, neither having been adopted, a number of new dogs had come and occupied the other spaces around Toby. There was Leonard, a squat, loud hunting dog who sat across from him and howled incessantly at the smallest noise. There was also Ruby, her coat a rich chocolate and her size and build reminding Toby of old Zeke. Ruby was gray at the muzzle too, but her gait was young and fluid; she looked like she would run for days. Whenever Ruby would be taken for a walk, she would stop at Toby's gate and beckon for him to touch noses, seemingly hoping to pass on her buoyant spirits to the young dog.

After many days, Toby's lethargy morphed into frustration, brewing into an anxious and insatiable energy. He would pace back and forth in his kennel, side to side and front to back. Sometimes he would knock at his water bowl with his paws, spilling water on the concrete and staining his paws. As people would pass his gate, he would approach and bark loudly, commanding them to pay attention to him. At the smallest acknowledgment, his paws would rise to the gate and he would fixate on their eyes.

When he did not like a visitor, he would bark deeply with an occasional low growl interspersed with his commotion. When Roland would visit with his hose, Toby would stand defiantly, now growling steadily at the old man, only breaking his intense stare long enough to turn his head from the spray of cold water. Even Derrick received the occasional growl, the young dog seemingly drawn back to his resentment over the fates of Oscar and Julius. While Derrick remained patient through the outbursts, it pained him gravely to watch Toby breaking before his eyes.

Only Anne seemed to be able to rouse the old Toby. She spent every free moment of her day sitting in front of or even in his kennel, wrapping her arms around him, combing him with a soft brush, or just generally talking to him softly.

And so the weeks of a long winter passed. Toby

had been at the shelter for a long four months now. While other dogs came and went, he had not received a single application, and only a handful of people had even expressed interest in him.

Anne tried everything she knew to get him out of this place. In her fracturing heart, she hoped that her efforts would matter somehow. She hoped that something she did would be the path to a better place for him. She made him a fancy new kennel card for him with bright fluorescent colors and pictures of happier times. She made sure that all of the volunteers knew that Toby was a top priority. She even put out a plea to everyone she knew, hoping to find a foster home for him, even for a short time. No one was able or willing.

In time, Dizzy was adopted and the kennel next to Toby grew cold and empty, the scuttling of claws on the concrete and the cheerful barks were gone, replaced only by a dull stillness. Only Jack remained by Toby's side, but he was growing older and more tired despite the detached front he put forth. Toby felt like the walls were caving in on him and his already tiny cell was growing smaller and smaller.

Toby's plight was hard on the shelter staff. They often wore long faces and spoke in hushed tones around him, their faces drawn with concern. Anne in particular felt that she had failed Toby. Her experiment at fostering him had shown great promise, but she was unable to see it through. If she weren't so poor, she would have a home of her own and be free from the ridiculous rules of her apartment complex.

One day, Susan approached her in the break room.

"Anne, I'm sorry, but we're probably going to have to move Toby off of the Adoption floor if this continues. He's growled at three separate people this week," she said, her tone sincerely apologetic.

Anne was silent. There was nothing to say. She would just try harder. As she sat in the worn, black office chair finishing her morning coffee, she looked out the window to the empty play yard and wondered to herself. Where was his adopter? Why couldn't someone just see his true spirit? She knew deep down that Toby had always had an uphill climb. He was black. He was a pit bull mix. And he was in a shelter. But despite it all, she knew that if somehow he could just get out and be free of this place, he would flourish.

Desperately, Anne reached out to all of her dog rescue contacts, calling in favors and pleading with people. Her spirits lifted for a moment when she got one rescue group to agree to send a volunteer to come meet him. But Toby was hyper in the play yard, wild and unresponsive to commands or direction. He jumped on the volunteer, snatching the toy from her hand and racing manically around the play yard. They didn't have any place for him, the volunteer told Anne. There were many other dogs who would fit better into their open foster home and it just wouldn't work out, she said. Anne was frustrated, but she understood. The shelter was full of dozens of other dogs who were holding up better than Toby.

One afternoon, Derrick came to Anne and motioned for her to come with him into the break room. She followed him, noticing a look of dejection on his face. As the door closed behind them, Derrick pulled his hand from his pocket to reveal two fresh punctures set in a smear of fresh blood. Anne covered her mouth with her tiny hand and whispered, "Toby?"

Derrick simply nodded.

"How?" she said.

"Opened the gate to lift up his water bowl and he snapped at me. No growl, nothing," said Derrick, his voice melancholy with a hint of compassion.

Anne's hand remained on her mouth. Her eyes began to water. Derrick walked past her, placing his other hand briefly on her shoulder and then went to find a towel to dry the blood. She stood motionless for a long minute, her mind spiraling, the guilt beginning to bubble inside her again.

She slept little that night, tossing and turning, her mind racing, replaying the events of that day. She thought of the conversation with Derrick. She stirred as she remembered the staff meeting that followed with the somber faces and the tears that flowed freely from her and Melissa. She remembered Derrick's warm embrace as he wrapped his big arm around her shoulder and pulled her close, speaking quietly in her ear.

"We did everything we could." His voice was tender and consoling, but still the pain would not leave her.

She thought back to the time with Toby in her

apartment, how much he and Brutus had enjoyed each other and how much he had thrived. In her mind, as she lay there in the blackness, she could envision the letter from the apartment complex. She could feel the paper in her hands as she read the cruel writing. She thought about Oscar and Julius and the injustice of their lives.

And she thought for a long time about Toby. He hadn't come to them broken like Oscar or Julius. He had come with promise: a young family dog eager for the home that he deserved. The place had broken him: the concrete walls, the constant wailing noises and clanking of pans, the long days in his kennel — they were the end of him. Staring upwards at the wobbling circle of her ceiling fan, Anne thought about the count-less hours they spent working with him, showing him how much they cared for him, constantly searching for an answer for him and trying, most of all, to keep him from the abyss. None of it mattered in the end. Their bravest efforts couldn't appease the hungry shelter from consuming him.

As the hours drew on, her tired mind turned un-willingly towards tomorrow and she began to play the day through her head. She pushed the thoughts away, deeper into her mind; she wasn't going to think about that now. She filled the space in her mind by replaying how she had left Toby earlier that day. She had packed him the largest rubber chew toy she could find, filled to the brim with peanut butter and dog biscuits. Her hands were slathered and sticky with peanut butter by the time she was finished. She had crawled in his kennel on her hands and knees and spread out a soft, warm blanket across his plastic bed. Then she had sat there with him in the shadows. Toby was suddenly happy to have company and licked her face, placing his paws on her lap. She sat there and cried, the tears streaming down her face as Toby hurried to clean them from her cheek with his tongue. Despite his best efforts, the tears wouldn't stop, spilling forth to the cold, concrete floor.

Anne turned and looked at the clock. It was 4:34AM and she had to be up in two hours. She hadn't slept a wink, but she rose from bed, accepting that she would not sleep this night. She put on her slippers and walked to the sofa. The shuffling of footsteps followed her as Brutus rose from his bed on the floor. Anne slowly clambered onto the sofa, sitting cross-legged. Brutus, yawning and stretching the tiredness from his lanky frame followed her, crawling into her lap with a sigh and curled himself into a ball. She wrapped both hands around him and buried her head in his fur.

Just a few short hours later, Anne arrived at the shelter as a fine mist of rain saturated the air. The sun cowered behind a drab blanket of gray clouds. She parked in her usual spot and opened the door to enter. As she did, she noticed her battered old car rolled forward into the curb, her mind elsewhere, having forgotten to shift the vehicle to park. She climbed in and pushed forward on the shifter. Her chin touched her chest as she slouched back in the seat, savoring the extra moments. After a minute, another vehicle pulled in next to her and she lifted her head at the sound of a car door shutting.

"Come on, girl," spoke Derrick, giving her a gentle pat to coax her from the car.

She pulled the keys from the ignition and slid from the car, a half-lifeless form avoiding eye contact with Derrick. He closed the door behind her, and the two walked through the doors of the shelter, side by side, tears once again welling in her eyes.

Melissa was at the desk as they entered. She gave a brief look at the pair and her mouth turned to a frown as their eyes connected. Behind her, Roland was passing with a mop bucket, already started on the morning chores.

Anne shuffled over and noted her timecard robotically and then took a seat next to Melissa. She flipped on the computer, attempting to find some work to take her mind off of what the day held, but after several minutes, she again rested her head on her chin and sat blankly. There was nothing else of consequence today and she knew it. There was no point stalling or postponing the inevitable. The shelter was closed today; there would be no visitors, no rescue groups coming to look at dogs, nothing at all that could possibly save him.

She gathered her strength and rose from her seat. Derrick had moved to the back of the shelter. Anne keyed the intercom. "Derrick to Euth, please," she said, the words hanging heavy in the air as they crackled across the wires of the old communication system.

She held the microphone for a moment and then placed it back on the table. Melissa was still keying away on the computer, but she turned and cast a look at Anne and then reached to pat her on the leg as she moved away.

After several minutes, the back door opened, and Derrick came through. His eyes were red which was something Anne could not recall having ever seen before. She looked away out of respect for the gentle man and moved towards the door that led to the Euthanasia Room.

Derrick followed behind and the two of them said nothing as Anne opened the medicine cabinet with her keys and began to prepare the injection. Derrick wiped down the table with a spray bottle and white cloth and then aimlessly straightened objects in the room as Anne worked.

"I'll go get him," he said as Anne continued her preparations in stoic solitude.

"No, I will," she replied, sharper than she intended. "But thank you," she followed to soften her tone, patting Derrick on the arm as she passed.

The walk to the kennels was a blur of dulled concrete, faded metal, barking dogs, and a swirling sickness in her stomach. Anne's whole body was trembling. A sense of nausea filled her gut, and she felt as sad as she could ever recall. As she opened the kennel doors, the ruckus of sounds stirred her back to attention, and she shuffled her way to Toby's kennel, not even glancing at the other dogs who tried vainly to gain her attention.

Toby was at the gate with a sudden lunge, but he backed down when he recognized Anne. He stood upright, his tail wagging comfortably now. Anne thought he looked suddenly regal as if he was the king of this dark castle. She looked into his eyes, admiring him, seeing what everyone else who passed him by never would. He tilted his head slightly to the right, sensing Anne's emotions. The wag of his tail slowed, pensive now. Anne dipped her head and broke eye contact with Toby. The tears rolled from her eyes, dripping to the floor and mixing as one with the thin residue of soap and water on the concrete. Toby let out a yip to try and stem the tears. Anne lifted at the collar of her smock and wiped her eyes. A faint smile formed on her face as she looked again at Toby who was staring back at her. The deep yellow of his eyes shone brilliantly in the shadows of the kennel.

"I'm sorry, big fella," she said, her false smile fading again. "We really, really tried," she said.

And with that, her hand moved to the latch on the kennel and lifted.

Toby looked at the open gate and hesitated. His natural urge to rush through the opening for a walk or some time in the play yard was tempered. He stood for some time, glancing back and forth between Anne's face and the open gate before him. Anne crouched down and motioned for Toby to come to her. He took one slow step forward and then stopped again, studying her face. She smiled another false smile. He took two more halting steps forward, his eyes brimming with concern. Anne reached forward and took his collar under her fingers, clipped the leash to the metal clasp, and then rose, standing now in the small puddle of her tears.

Walking swiftly in a near-trot, both to encourage Toby forward and to hasten this dismal event, Anne led the young dog out of the kennel. Behind him, unseen to either, Jack stood at the front of his gate, keeping a quiet and somber vigil. Several kennels away, Leonard bayed a long, mournful howl.

The door opened swiftly, jolting Derrick to attention. Anne entered with Toby close behind. The young dog stopped at the doorway and planted his feet firmly on the bottom of the door stop, the grave smells of the room rushing into him like some rotten gale. His eyes grew wide and scared, and he began to quiver and shake uncontrollably, his pupils darting across the room.

Anne made only a half-hearted attempt to move him forward, but it wasn't in her. Once again, she bowed her head and began to cry. Across the small room, Derrick laid down a syringe and moved to help her. His voice was calm and smooth as he tried to comfort both Toby and Anne with his words.

He reached out with his hand, searching for the crook behind Toby's ear to give some gentle, reassuring strokes. Toby's eyes were wild, and his tail was tucked deeply underneath him, almost invisible. He hunkered low against the ground just outside the doorway as Derrick's hand moved closer.

And then Toby snapped, his jaws gnashing upwards, searching vainly for Derrick's hand which he quickly pulled back just in time. Toby sank further into the concrete, his lips curled. The whites of his eyes were bright over his wrinkling nose.

Behind him, Anne's hands gently caressed the length of his back. She soothed him, her voice gentle now, suddenly absent of fear. Toby continued to shake, but Anne pressed onwards, fighting valiantly against her emotions to vanquish his fear in these critical moments.

"It's ok, baby. I know you're scared. It's going to be ok," she repeated over and over and over again. The guilt of her false words wounded her.

Gently, she pressed her hands underneath Toby and paused for a moment, hugging him, unabated by any fears of his reaction. The warmth of his body soaked through her smock, absorbing deep into her soul. She could feel the rapid thumping of his heart. She could feel the life in him, the possibilities.

Pushing these thoughts from her mind, she stood, battling against her unconscious desires, and bent her legs, lifting him onto the metal table. The cool chill of steel felt awkward and unjust against the warmth of the vibrant young dog. Toby lay down on the table, somewhat calmed in the embrace of Anne's wispy arms. Her mouth pressed against his ears, and her soft words subdued him as Derrick carefully placed a mesh muzzle over his snout without protest.

Derrick stepped back and looked at Anne, his expression asking a clear question. She shook her head back and forth and gestured him away. She would do this herself. Her hand slid under Toby and braced against his right forearm. He sat motionless, trusting fully in Anne, the best friend he had ever known. His shaking had mostly stopped, and his breathing was calm. Anne twisted the skin of his forearm with her thumb, exposing the vein.

Toby didn't even feel the first needle go in; he only realized a sudden, cold rush of liquid up his arm and into his chest. He sat there motionless, his mind given completely to the love of Anne's embrace. And then he grew very tired, so very, very tired. His head began to bob and dip as he fought to stay awake. He could feel her tender touch under his chin, guiding his head to the table. From the corner of his eye, he saw Derrick move forward with a folded towel, and felt his chin rest on its cloth.

He could hear Anne's words. They sounded distant from some far-off world, as if from the blue skies well beyond the walls of this place.

"I'm so, so sorry, Toby," she said. He could hear her crying. "We tried our best... I'm so sorry that none of it mattered in the end," she said, her voice breaking from a place beyond his senses.

Toby didn't understand the words, but he knew what they meant. Deep in the furthest recesses of his fading heart, he knew exactly what she had said. As the fog of a deep slumber drew across his weary mind, he wished only that he could speak to her, to cross the great divide so that she could hear him and understand him.

"But it did," he said in his mind.

And then Toby fell to an eternal sleep, his spirit filled absolute at that moment with the serene beauty that surrounded him, this final kindness chasing the darkness to the farthest corners of his mind.

And he was free.

# EPILOGUE

Every year across the United States, millions of dogs find themselves frightened and alone in public or private animal shelters. Each of them arrives in their own way. Some have been surrendered by former owners, others have been picked up roaming the streets as strays, and those less fortunate have been seized from situations of abject cruelty or neglect.

Despite the thankless, heroic efforts of devoted staff and volunteers, hundreds of thousands of them will never leave the shelter alive.

Behind every lonely bark that resonates down the long, cold halls is a story.

Behind the clatter of every stainless steel bowl on the barren floor is a vibrant, rich life, longing to be lived.

Behind every frightened whimper from the shadowy corner of a concrete alcove is a story of redemption, waiting to be written.

This book tells the story of one such life, but across our country, there are countless dogs like Toby, Jack, Marilynn, Oscar, Julius, Dizzy, and the others in these pages. Some sit in shelters now, from Virginia to California and everywhere in between. Others will find their way through the doors in the days and years to come.

Dogs hold a very special place in our society, ingrained in the fabric of America. Yet their position in our lives is both blessing and curse. For some, the very traits that endear them to us — loyalty, companionship, and love without condition — cause them to be abused, neglected, or even fought against each other. We have fallen in love with dogs and in doing so, we have also forsaken them.

Our world is incredibly diverse and complicated. Yet amongst our achievements and excesses, there is nothing as pure and unquestionably righteous as the love of the simplest dog. Even the most worn, neglected, and downtrodden of their species possesses a capacity for affection and forgiveness that belittles our greatest attributes.

For everything they give to us, we owe them so much more.

# ABOUT THE AUTHOR

**WILL LOWREY** is an attorney and animal rights advocate from Richmond, Virginia. He holds a Juris Doctor from Vermont Law School and a Bachelor of Science from Virginia Commonwealth University. Will has been actively involved in animal causes for over 15 years, including experiences with animal sheltering, pit bull advocacy, natural disaster response, animal fighting cases, roadside zoo closures, Native American reservations, community outreach, protests, and public records campaigns. He is also the author of "We the Pit Bull: The Fate of Pit Bulls Under the United States Constitution" published in the *Lewis and Clark Animal Law Review Journal, Volume 24, Issue 2.*

For comments, questions, copyright, or ordering information, visit **lomackpublishing.com**